The Year That Followed

a novel

By

Thomas Andrews

Manufactured by CreateSpace

2016 – by Thomas Andrews
Associate ed. Miss Shayna Sommers
Grateful acknowledgement is handed to those who read and assisted the author in the creation of this work.

First Paperback Edition – April 2016

ISBN-13: 978-1532827839
ISBN-10: 1532827830

Also by Thomas Andrews:

Type: Writer *a Novel - 2014*

For those who choose to look ahead.

I - June 16ᵗʰ – Jonathan

Jonathan could not remember what the argument – or fight – was even about as they walked to the car. It had gone on for so long it had just become something and nothing. Fiona was probably angrier than he was, but she was also probably right about what had first ticked off this particular bout. As most fights or arguments do, this one had a quiet spell. The period was filled with an awkward silence broken only by the loud voice in the two heads in the car telling them that it was all ridiculous and that they shouldn't even be angry. The voice was particularly loud for Jonathan. He felt awful for several of the things he had said in the preceding shouting matches but knew Fiona knew there had been no sincerity in his words. Such was the case for the things she had said to him in a brief fit of rage for something he had probably done. He knew she loved him and was feeling the same things in her head as he was.

- I'm sorry.
- I know it's fine, so am I.

Such mutual apologies rarely concluded those sorts of bouts, but in this case it did enough to relieve some of the pressure and silence the animals within their heads to a lesser drone while they drove on through the late evening. Jonathan was still feeling the sharp tangs of the dinner he had eaten earlier on the corners of his mouth and around his lips. It was spicier than usual. Fiona had done something different or added

4

something to it — he couldn't remember or place the taste. As he wiped his mouth with his hand she motioned with her head.

- It was a bit hotter this time wasn't it. I don't really know why to be honest.
- Yea it was still really good though.

Several small conversations like that seemed to be enough to patch up the various damaged areas in their minds as the miles ticked down and they neared Alex and Tom's. He tried to recall if it was meant to be a big group that night or if it was just going to be the four of them. Alex had a habit of inviting extra guests at the last minute that nobody in the "core group" of friends really knew that well so everyone had to spend the evening introducing themselves and telling their life stories over and over again. This was, in a way, fairly detrimental to the evening's conversation as it would usually progress to actual topics rather than life synopses when it was just close friends. Either way, it had been a long time since they had gone to see Alex and Tom like this so it was good to be getting out. It was even better to be patching things up to a workable level in the car rather than entering the house with a fairly icy no-man's-land still present between them.

Jonathan rounded the corner on the country road leading away from town and Fiona had broken the barrier at last. She placed her hand gently on his as it rested atop the gearstick. He knew her, though. This was by no means an admission of guilt, a truce, or a concession to being wrong. She just loved him and it was the right time to show it. He lifted his thumb gently and reached it back towards her hand and touched her back gently as he drove. She knew the road as well as he and gently released the pressure she put on his hand just before she knew he would have to change gear; she knew too well that he would try to shift as infrequently as possible so as to keep her hand in contact with his own at all times.

- I love you.
- I know, this will be fun tonight. Let's hope Alex hasn't invited the whole neighborhood again.

He laughed a little.

- Yea. Wishful thinking though, probably.

The drive was nice and familiar even though he hadn't taken the last few roads since the last time they had been out to Tom and Alex's place some time ago. The sun was completely down as they drew nearer and he was about ready for a glass of wine or one of Tom's beers. Fiona looked awfully beautiful in her sun dress and sandals. Her legs were crossed out in front of her in the passenger seat as she looked out of her window and slightly upwards as though with a hint of excitement or wonder in what she beheld – her hand remained upon his as she gazed out of the window. He took his eyes off of her briefly to focus on the road as they rounded a few more turns.

The animals from the earlier row now slept quietly in the back seat of each of their minds as Jonathan did his best to keep the ride smooth until they arrived.

The radio broke the silence – that was not uncomfortable in and of itself – and lent a little insight into some sort of political issue gripping the minds of many for a few short minutes before the next came along to otherwise occupy such thoughts. Jonathan's work at the university often called for him to be much more active than he was regarding such issues. He took offense to the implication that he was in any way uninvolved but never voiced it. Fiona always knew much more than she let on and surprised everyone greatly at parties when she could hold her own against even the loudest of ignorant pseudo-intellectuals not expecting a contender. He loved it.

"Seven people have been confirmed dead in Istanbul in the latest bombing in Turkey's capital…"

"Latest attacks considered to be related to the string of bombings in central Europe over the past 6 months, however, no group has come forward yet to claim responsibility. This leads to the growing belief and concern that militant-behaviour has been inspired in civilians as some form of copycat activity…"

The phrase "no news is good news" passed briefly through Jonathan's mind as he drove, but, in many ways he simply felt lucky that he was unaffected by such issues. His mind wandered and such thoughts eventually led to some form of guilt for feeling so content.

- They haven't done food have they?

He was immediately worried about the fact that they had already eaten and would possibly have to navigate either an awkward dinner in which neither of them ate their share or a potentially more awkward rejection of whatever was prepared while trying to be polite.

- I don't know actually. Alex usually likes to do something. I guess it depends on who's going. If there's a big group, it won't matter and we can just take a little, I guess.

Jonathan was comforted by Fiona's reasoning. She was on the same side as he was and hated the awkward confrontation that might ensue. It would be fine. It was going to be a decent evening regardless. The wine really was seeming like a great idea at this point and they were nearly there.

Fiona pulled her summer scarf over her legs as the darkness beyond the car made it seem cooler than it was despite the summer air. Jonathan turned the heat on just a little in the car and she again placed her hand upon his without looking at him.

He liked being in the car with her.

2 - June 16th - Fiona

By the time they were ready to leave there was no ice left in Fiona's mind. Her temperament was that of her usual self: quiet, calm, and sincere with a look that many often mistook for vacancy if they found themselves staring at her face. She was glad that Jonathan was driving. It was nice that they would get to share the time of the drive together alone before the party. She was, however, really looking forward to spending some time with Alex and Tom as they lent some often needed comparative perspective for her life.

After sharing apologies, Fiona's mind wandered in the car while the radio was on. She thought about the holiday she'd taken with Jonathan several years earlier to Spain. It was a spur of the moment trip. It was unplanned; they left on the Wednesday having booked the trip on the Monday or something similar.

- I'm really looking forward to a trip like this for us.

Jonathan had said this after making the arrangements. It had certainly been in passing and was meant as a caring and obviously positive remark about his feelings for her. She had, of course, enjoyed spending her time on the beach with him while they pushed the limits of public indecency with their amorous behaviours under the illusion that if one is a tourist, he or she may do as they please. The trip was good. It was nice.

- I think I'm in love with you.

He had shared this with her during the trip for the first time. Despite her not having shared the sentiment back immediately, they both walked away from the situation relatively

8

emotionally unscathed and it did not take Fi – pronounced: *Fee,* or she would undoubtedly let you know - long to return the gesture.

The radio was shedding light on recent terrorist attacks. She quickly felt sad for those involved and ran a check in her mind for anyone she may know who had been in the area who may have been affected by the events. After coming up with nothing she relaxed a little into her seat and crossed her legs out in front of her. She was enjoying sharing this quiet time with Jonathan and showed her affection by gently holding his hand. It looked as though he needed it. He seemed to relax a little.

She liked to watch him while he was driving, or working, or when she knew that he could not tell that she was doing so. It was easy for her, but she knew that he was still bothered by their little spat from before they had left. It was nothing for him to worry about and she knew that he should know that. If anything, this made her more frustrated than whatever they had started up about. The vacancy in her stare was something she had found to be useful when watching Jonathan. She worried about him a lot but knew he was fine when it all came down to it. Fiona had always wondered why Jonathan had a habit of making things so complicated for himself in his mind. It was to her great relief that she knew she could alleviate his discomfort with just a touch or a few words.

Alex was, at this point, in the third year of her PhD studies at the University of Edinburgh. It looked as though it was going to take her another year after this one to complete her work. They had met a few years earlier at the university in the Special Collections department been close friends since. Alex was brilliant and remarkably down to earth. Fiona always tried to take an interest in her field and was particularly drawn to several of the comments she had made the last time they had talked on the phone.

- I've been interviewing this guy recently who thinks he's killed someone. He dreams about it and… just feels guilt, like, all the time.

The fact that she was still collecting her field notes showed how far off she was from finishing her degree.

- I can't work out what causes it with this guy. It cripples him, though. He's never been caught for doing anything and I am certain that he's by no means capable of harming anything, let alone killing someone.

Fiona had listened intently and immediately sympathized with the subject of Alex's story. She'd woken up with feelings of guilt. Obviously they had never manifested into confessions of guilt for acts that had not been committed, but she understood. Her ability to relate to others was uncanny and she had a way of sizing people up that would have been more likely suited to a much older woman.

While resting her hand atop Jonathan's on the gear stick, she looked carefully at his face. He caught the look and mouthed a small kiss without taking his eyes off the road. She saw him briefly catch the view of her legs in his peripherals and he stroked her hand with his thumb. He looked handsome for their night out but had a tiredness in his face that never seemed to leave him. He was two years younger than her at twenty-five, yet he carried himself as though he had shouldered the weight of at least an extra five. His hair, trimmed short to conceal the loss that was imminent, was dark brown even in the summer light. Fiona never thought of him as someone with a beard, but looking at his face she clocked the stubble and realized that she rarely saw him without it.

She wondered quickly at how he might have looked clean shaven. He was a big guy, perhaps contributing to the invisible weight shown in the early lines of his face. His eyes, in some lights, looked blue. On this evening they were their usual grey, full of thought as evidenced by the lines forming around them which would undoubtedly bloom into full view in his later years. His right hand rested firmly on the side of steering wheel at three-o'clock; the back of it revealing a roadmap of veins stretching and disappearing under his cuff. Displayed on alternate knuckles was the evidence of various accidents and scraps from previous years. Her hand remained covering his left. She felt safe. He was strong and solid.

- I'm glad you're coming with me to this tonight.

He looked over at her briefly.

- Why wouldn't I?

He smiled as he asked he question but he knew what she meant.

- I'm glad I get to go with you, too, darling.

Fiona knew where they were by this point. She prepared herself for the smiles and possible introductions if there happened to be a group of people there with whom she was unfamiliar. She pulled her scarf over her legs and watched as Jonathan adjusted the heat. The view from the window had changed from the countryside that she watched through glazed eyes and was now just the image of herself reflected back to her as the sun had completely disappeared. She adjusted her hair briefly as it fell loosely over her forehead and just dipped near to her eyes. Despite her usual reservations, she was happy with the way she looked on this occasion. They would go together well at Tom and Alex's; she was sure.

3 - June 16th Jonathan

Jonathan opened his eyes slowly and waited while they adjusted to the light. He explored the back of his head with one hand and felt a small trickle of blood creeping upwards from his neck towards the top of his head. He was upside-down, suspended in his seatbelt with the parachute material of the airbag dangling in his face now deflated. His knees rested on the bottom of the steering wheel which was now wrenched towards the right side of the car where the door was once intact. The breeze from the outside was calm and performed its duty of cooling the chaos of the situation. It highlighted the sting he felt in his back and up – or down – his neck.

Jonathan's mind was slow to click into gear. He was in his office. He was working on new materials for some upcoming program or other. The coffee on his desk was still warm. His seat was comfortable and the blinds were open allowing a stream of light to splay across the many pieces of unfinished work that were strewn around the room. While he typed at his computer and watched steam rise from the rim of his mug, he saw slow moving streams of thick, black-red ooze working their way down his forearms towards his fingers. They no longer did as they were told. His head began to throb as he tried his best to keep his composure while he worked. The steam no longer rose from his coffee and the light disappeared quickly allowing a grey hue to engulf the room and send what was technicolour back to black and white with the exception of the lines of red tracking down his wrists. His hands closed into clenched fists and his knuckles grew whiter from the pressure.

The wind now cooled the entire office and began to stir the various pages of the open books about the room. The noise of the pages fluttering became louder and louder until it

12

was impossible to ignore and he could no longer work. *Fiona, babe. Can you close the windows in the kitchen for me? I'm getting a draft...*" As his hands had refused to work first, so now did his mouth. A dryness like hair in his throat culled any chance of being noticed. His call could not be heard and he found himself rooted to his chair in his darkening office becoming colder; unable to speak. He could hear Fiona walking around down the hall.

- FUCK. Oh shit. What the fuck... happened.

Jonathan's mind snapped quickly back to the car. His head throbbed in agony as he spewed profanity at his situation. The blood dripping towards his fingers seemed to begin at each elbow from the impact or the glass as the car had flipped and slid across the road on its roof. The gash in his upper back was worryingly deep and, he thought, probably pretty close to some important stuff. He wiggled his toes – which were above him in the upside down vehicle – and knocked free some shards of glass which fell through the steering wheel and landed painlessly on his face.

- HEY! FIONA!

He called violently and heard the tone in his voice. It was a tone of frightened panic that he had not heard from himself in a long time. Whatever calmness he had cultivated in recent years had quickly left him. Turning his head at this point was out of the question thanks to the bastard of a gash in his back leading to the large stain forming in his hair. Blood was now choosing a path; stretching its way like a necklace around each side of his neck and into his beard.

- Fiona I can't move my head! Are you ok? Fi?

It was hard to hear too much outside of his own head as the wind was getting stronger and louder outside of the car. The engine was no longer running but still released sounds indicative of mechanical pain. Fiona didn't respond.

- Fiona? Darling? We have to get out of the car. It's upside down so it could catch fire really fucking easily. We have to get out. Okay?

Again the call fell on deaf ears.

The pain in his back felt electrical. A slight move in his head led to a shocking sensation down his spine that almost caused him to black out each time. His shouts made the pain worse, but he had to get out of the car. The injuries to his arms causing the blood to spread seemed relatively superficial and he couldn't feel the wounds themselves as he reached to click himself from his seatbelt. After groping for several seconds without looking down — or up — to where the clasp was, he stopped his actions abruptly. If he simply clicked out of his belt, he was sure to land upon his head with the full weight of his body coming down upon him. With this in mind, he braced his right hand against the roof of the car — which was much closer to the top of his head than it had once been — and carefully released the belt.

As he fell sideways and landed awkwardly upon more glass and twisted metal he saw two things. One: the cause of the injury to his back. Two: Fiona was not in the passenger seat where she should have been. The triangular shaped shard of racing green-tinted and bloodstained metal protruding through the back of the driver's seat about four inches below the headrest had most likely come from the frame of the back door when the car flipped onto its roof. Had it come through further Jonathan would have undoubtedly been killed on the spot. He shifted his eyes back to the empty passenger seat and his mind — now functioning at a rapid speed apparently making up for his earlier lapse — thought of the possibilities that could have occurred during the crash.

A small dip in the road combined with a front left tire deciding to burst at just under sixty miles an hour had caused the car to lurch forward onto the rim and flip immediately on to its roof. The chair that had previously cradled Fiona's small frame now hung empty from the floor of the car just above Jonathan's head. *She must have got out before I came to. She's already out of the car and I just can't hear her.* He felt relieved at this thought and did his best to shuffle backwards out of the open space where the door had come off. The motion in his neck was still limited and the electrical shocks that he felt going down his spine were more frequent; he was in agony. What he felt, though, was not the wincing and convulsing that his body was doing involuntarily, but rather the excitement that Fiona had broken free from the mangled metal and glass cage that had once been their 3-Series and was undoubtedly waiting for him just a few yards away; probably calling his name. He could not hear her for the noise of the summer wind over the hills, but he was sure she would be there.

She was. As Jonathan moved a few feet away from the wreckage he felt the cool grass against his stomach which told him the car had made it off the road in the accident; at least half of it anyway. The windshield faced up the road in the direction they had been moving, but he couldn't be sure how the car had rolled or turned during the incident itself. Despite the throbbing in his head and the impairment this was clearly causing his vision, he saw Fiona waiting for him no more than 30 feet away from him. *If I've been out for a while by now, then Alex and Tom will be wondering where we are…they will call or send someone…they know the way we drive in…unless they have invited thirty fucking people like last time.* Unable to stand, but with newfound excitement and adrenaline coursing through him like he had never felt before, Jonathan pulled himself rapidly along the road in a quasi-military style using his toes to push in his boots and pulling fiercely with all the might in his arms to the point that his fingertips each opened small grazes and bled slightly along the way.

- Fuck. FUCK! She's alright. FIONA! Fiona. Get up. You're alright.

His words, though loud and fierce, had no resonance in the wind and he was left screaming only to himself as he neared her body. She lay gently on her front with her legs bent slightly upwards towards her chest as though she was sleeping like a child. The scarf once draped over her legs to keep warm in the summer evening continued its duties as it had become wrapped around her thighs and waist; it was darkened and wadded with a black and red mixture and clung to her body tightly. Jonathan felt tears welling up but was struck and overcome by anger and pain and quickly blacked out upon reaching her in the road. Her face, while serene in expression and untarnished or bloodstained like Jonathan's, was severely blackened on her left side by the impact that had taken her life.

The face that had come to permeate his life was no longer the one that looked back to him. The vacant brown eyes that contained so much more than most people ever gave credit for were half open as though dazed. Her short hair – it had once stretched beautifully down her back but was now kept short in a "bob" style cut – was matted against her forehead as she lay on the cool tarmac. It usually hung just enough in her eyes for her to perpetually look up slightly as though she was far more interested in what was going on around her than she actually was; otherwise she was forever flipping her hair back and out of her eyes. Jonathan thought about her yoga while resting next to her. *Would she be able to do the things she loved anymore?* He looked up and down her body and recalled every time he had extolled its many virtues and outlined its perfections during her times of self-doubt. Placing his hand very gently on her hip while he lay next to her, he closed his eyes and breathed out a small cough and sputter.

Had the wind calmed, the sound of the approaching ambulance and fire-engine would have been heard at the crash site.

---

4 - June 19th – Jonathan

- Mr. Eliot. Your wife's injuries in the accident killed her immediately. When the ambulance arrived you had been unconscious for some time. You may remember some of the events from directly after the crash.
- I was awake. I know.

Jonathan did not look at the doctor while he spoke. His eyes merely gazed blankly at the opaque window as the white sunlight struggled to make its way through.

- You've lapsed in and out of consciousness over the past few days, it's good to see that you are awake and responding well today.

This is total bullshit. First thing he says to me when I wake up is that my wife is dead.

The doctor continued explaining Jonathan's situation in a monotone voice surely meant to convey condolence or compassion; it only made things worse. Much of what he was saying had apparently already been said to Jonathan while he had been awake a day or so earlier, but he had no recollection of such conversations having ever happened. He wondered if this was because he had simply blocked out the knowledge of everything that had happened or if his injuries had caused this blackout effect.

17

Jonathan walked around the house aimlessly the first time that Fiona had almost left him. Eating had become nothing but a means of not losing too much weight until his feelings of anxiety passed. He forced down meals for three days while she figured things out.

- I can't imagine anyone ever making me as happy as you do.

She had meant it when she said it, but there was a great deal of concern in her voice, too.

- I'm scared, for sure. I just want to make sure *now* that this is what I should be doing. If I wait too long, it'll be worse.
- For sure... There's no doubt in my mind about what I want. There's clearly doubt in yours and that's a pretty big concern... You know I just want to make you happy, though.

It was a conversation they would have so many times throughout their relationship and even after they were married. It hurt Jonathan every time, but he found new ways of dealing with the situation and putting out fires along the way. He knew she loved him.

They would spend time with friends afterwards, Tom and Alex would be over periodically with beers and so many stories from work and school. Jonathan would do his best to show that he had learned from the mistakes leading up to each difficult spell, but more so he would work to show that he was in the same frame of mind as Fiona. Eventually such spells became the norm and they became practiced at working through them. They caused him less pain as he rationalized the situation as something that was just part of the relationship that had to be dealt with rather than something that had the power to derail their lives. After each spell of uncertainty, he had become adept at blocking the events from his mind.

What was said last, that was all that mattered. As long as nothing had happened that could change the fabric of what they had on a fundamental level, he could move on and deal with his work as a 'relationship counsellor' for the two of them.

Such duties once inspired him to bring her home a gift for no reason whatsoever. He had picked out a fountain pen coupled with a small bottle of ink and finished the gesture with a small notebook with blank, unlined pages. Fi was by no means a writer, but she was sentimental and intelligent.

- You're going to make me cry!
- Don't say that, I do that enough already for the wrong reasons, don't I?

She gently pawed at his arm and looked up at him in thanks.

- I really like it. I have to think of things to write now, though!
- It doesn't matter if you don't use it. I won't be offended; I just saw the stuff the other day and it looked like something you might like.
- It is. And I will use it.

Such occasions were the times when Jonathan felt as though he was able to give more back to Fiona than simply quelling her concerns. He was able to make her feel special in the way that he couldn't always convey.

Abruptly he was back in the hospital bed being spoken at by the monotonous doctor. *Has anyone been to visit me yet? I have so goddamn much to do right now… I have to sort everything out…* The machine recording his heart rate began to beep faster so as to illustrate his stress in a visual and audible manifestation. He began sweating more and he felt the sheets beneath his back begin to stick to him in the various places where his skin remained un-bandaged. After some time, the doctor had stopped speaking and left the room without any acknowledgement or signal from Jonathan. This was the first time that he had thought about his own condition and tried to move his head to take a look at his body and evaluate his own injuries. His head swiveled on its axis and moved reluctantly, with a stiff and abrasive slide as though two pieces of unpolished wood were forced to brush against each other. Such movements felt almost detached from himself. He suspected that this was due to an abundance of painkillers and would later find out that such a suspicion was right on the money. From the waist down, it appeared as though he had very little to be concerned about other than just a few scratches. The gash on his back, as he had thought, appeared to be the most significant injury he'd sustained, and now that he could move his head he was sure that he would make a full recovery relatively quickly. He felt sick while thinking about his own injuries while his wife was sure to be lain haphazardly on a metal tray in some large drawer several floors below where his room was in the hospital with an uncomfortable tag tied around her toe with brown string. He imagined the blue-grey hue of the room in which she lay and his eye seemed to adjust to such a tone in his present surroundings. The sun dipped slightly behind a cloud beyond the opaque glass of his window and the gloom increased.

Jonathan's arms were both in plaster. His "gauntlet style" white cuffs stretched from his knuckles to about an inch before his elbow, he suspected he would not be rallying for people to sign them like last time.

- Damn it Jonathan. I told you. I literally told you before we left the house tonight not to get too silly.
- I know, right!

He was drunk in the back of a taxi next to a pissed-off looking Fiona while they drove home from the hospital. His cast was still warm after having broken his arm running down the street in a drunken state on the evening of his twenty-third birthday.

- Are you still going to be able to work? You won't be able to go to the gym for ages now.

She outlined the various limitations on their drive home in the taxi but he knew she was more concerned rather than angry. Throughout the evening he had apologized to her for being silly enough to get hurt in the first place, but they'd both had a good night regardless. The three-hour stint in the hospital only lent perspective towards how drunk they had both been by the fact that it was only one-thirty in the morning by the time they were getting home. Jonathan's fall must have come very early in the evening. He felt held her hand in his broken hand in the back of the cab with a thumbless grip.

- You probably wont want me to hold your hand with this one much after today.
- Why's that?
- Well I'm not going to be able to wash it all that well. When I broke my other wrist as a kid it got pretty stinky after a few weeks in the sun.
- That's gross Jonathan!

She batted his arm away and he feigned pain to make her feel bad and they stayed close to each other for the remainder of the drive. He watched her as she looked out of the window and gently rubbed her thumb over the fingers that poked out of the end of his cast.

- At least you'll get everyone to sign them at the university.

Her remark was made with a little smirk as she remained looking out of the window. She had been right. After just a few days there was very little white real estate remaining as students and faculty alike had strewn their graffiti and profanity all the way along it. Reuben had even been sensible enough to draw the outline of a cock and balls in the palm so that Jonathan would be caressing it for the whole time he wore the cast. It was hard to believe that they had been in their twenties sometimes.

Jonathan gazed blankly at the casts on each of his wrists and thought about Reuben, his parents, Fiona's mum, Alex and Tom, and everyone else that he was going to have to see very shortly. It was too much. He closed his eyes in the hospital and tried to go back to the taxi with Fiona while she scolded him like a child. She had always lauded her two years of seniority over him in situations like that and he loved it. However tight he closed his eyes he couldn't get back there and the throbbing in his head from thinking too much became too much to bear. He released his eyelids, allowing a slow stream to fall from each eye upon opening, and stared emptily at the ceiling.

---

5 - August 24th – Jonathan

Work was finally beginning to take over for Jon. It occupied his mind in a fruitless effort to fill the shotgun-blast-sized hole in his mind where Fiona had once lived. He made his coffee and sat at his desk immersed in the regulations and requirements for each course he had a hand in producing. He started with ideas and outlines, then drew on various classes he had taken years earlier for inspiration. He walked to the kitchen to make his coffee, drew two mugs from the cupboard and set the French press atop the counter. He scooped in the coffee grounds and waited for the water to boil. While he waited he put back one of the mugs and turned its handle to match with the rest in the cupboard for later use. He pressed his hands against the edge of the counter and leant over the coffee press. The smell was comforting for a brief moment before the low, dull ache in his wrists brought him back to the moment. His casts had come off the week before, but there was still some residual pain that he was working through despite the overabundance of painkillers he was washing down with each coffee every day. Once again drawing another cup from the cupboard and pouring hot water over the grounds to break the seal he fetched cream from the fridge and got a spoon out for the sugar.

Jon's phone was ringing on his desk in his office. He heard it vibrate and play his generic ringtone meaning he didn't know who was calling. It rang off while he poured the coffee; cream and sugar for him, just cream for Fiona. He stepped a few steps towards the living room with Fiona's coffee in hand and turned and launched it across the room watching it smash and create a boiling brown mess dripping down the beige paintwork and staining the carpet.

- Fuck's sake.

He said it quietly. The first time. Then yelled it much more loudly and slammed his now empty hand against the wall in frustration. The twinge of pain at his actions would usually have been enough to piss him off further but he instead sat down in his place and held his coffee. As he slid his back down the front of the refrigerator on his way to the ground he felt the unfamiliar bumps and lines of his scar glide over the surface beneath his shirt. After sitting until his coffee was sufficiently cool enough to drink and wiping the salt water from his eyes he stood and gathered paper towels to begin cleaning his mess.

Geoffrey walked into the house after having rung the doorbell a few times and called Jon's name. Earlier he had tried his cell phone but apparently Jon had developed a new habit of using his phone as nothing more than a paperweight good for making noise and occasionally lighting up its surroundings.

- What on earth are you doing mate?
- What does it look like?
- Looks like you made a pretty good mess and then had a pretty shite go at cleaning it up.

Geoffrey stood looking down at his son who remained on all fours brushing coffee into the carpet with paper towels.

- Yea. I dropped my coffee.

Geoff looked at Jonathan's own cup of coffee resting on the side not 5 feet away. He touched the back of his fingers against it while looking down at his son, it was cold. He had been there for a while.

- Come on mate, up you get. Let's get out mate. Mum hasn't seen you in a while. Reuben came by the other day, too; said he couldn't reach you.
- Yea I've been busy cleaning. See?

Geoffrey walked slowly over to the couch, removed his jacket, and sat down breathing the heavy sigh that middle-aged guys have when they know they've earnt the right to do it.

- What are you doing here anyway?
- I came to see how you were. I'm not working at the moment anyway, it's too bloody windy to play golf. Your mum hasn't heard from you since—

Jon quickly interrupted. The last time he had seen most people except his dad – and reluctantly Reuben – was at Fiona's funeral.

- I know.

The first time Fiona had met Geoff and Clara had been a tense time for Jon. He sat quietly waiting for his cue in various family stories to corroborate or deny any particular events that his parents explained to Fiona. She listened quietly and took it in dutifully, asking questions when the situation called for it. Clara had thought, for most of Jon and Fiona's relationship, that her son's partner had not liked her. Fiona's vacancy in her look often had this effect on people. While most got over it quickly, Clara had struggled to build any sort of lasting relationship.

- I just think that she must find me so boring.
- Don't be silly, Mum.
- Well I don't know. Don't get me wrong Jonathan, you know I love Fiona.
- I know Mum. She loves you too, you know that. You don't have to be best friends either, though, just get along with each other; and you do. So that's fine.

Geoffrey, despite his reserved nature toward people his children knew, had clicked well with Fiona. Perhaps this was because Fiona's own father had not been around and he had felt a sense of responsibility towards her. Alternatively, Fi's seniority over Jon in her years had perhaps built a bridge between herself and Geoff based on their mutual passion for winding Jon up as much as possible. It was pretty easy to do and he seemed to rise to it so much more from his family than he did from Fiona, but when they teamed up it seemed almost unfair. Fiona's lack of expression allowed her to deliver a blow with little to no effort whatsoever before ultimately breaking down laughing with her father-in-law.

Geoff hauled himself from the sofa with the same groan that had placed him there some minutes earlier. He grabbed the paper towel from Jon's hands and issued a command this time.

- Get up. We're going out.

- Fine. Let me get changed. I can't be long either, I have so much goddamn work to do at the moment its ridiculous. Apparently nobody told me that "take all the time you need" just means "you'll have to catch it all up once you get back or you're fucked."
- Yea, well if you're that fucked a cup of tea and some fresh air isn't going to make a shred of difference. Is it?
- Okay.

They walked a short way from Jon's house to a nearby café for a drink. Neither expected that they would talk a great deal. It just was not yet time. Jon stared periodically at different points in his field of view, switching from his drink, to the sky just visible through the clouds out of the window, to the lines on his father's face across from him. *Will I look that way eventually?* Jon watched his dad tap his hand against the table, probably instinctively rather than for any purpose. His hand opened and closed slowly before he spoke each time.

- I don't know what anyone can say mate. I'm not about to sit here and explain to you how you're meant to feel or what you should have been doing since everything changed.
- Yea. I know man.

Geoff breathed a lot between his words and his statements. He sounded like a much older version of Jon's dad than he was used to.

- What are you going to do? What do you spend your time doing other than working at the moment?
- It's just work mate. I can't focus on anything else. Every time I seem to think about anything… it's like one of two things happens. Either I remember some awesome time for a few minutes or a few hours, get lost in it, and then come crashing back to now, or I

worry that the more I think about her the more she will just become some shit memory that I've created in my head for her rather than what she was. She seems to change every time I think about her.

They sat in silence and finished their drinks together after that. Both knew that there wasn't much to say. Geoff was still surprised that his son had returned to work so soon after Fiona had died.

Their walk home was, in fact, more helpful than the drink had been. It was doing Jon good to be outside. Unfortunately, it wouldn't take long to begin hurting for another reason. While Jon had enjoyed being outside in his youth and played sports throughout high school and university, he had never appreciated the landscape in the way that Fiona had. He had found it adorable at first. The way she looked at the world, to him, was as a child would behave on his first visit to a zoo or an aquarium. Her persistence in stopping him for countless photos of the sky or of a strange shaft of natural light eventually rubbed off on him despite his efforts for it not to.

- Scotland knows how to do the sky.

It was quiet when he spoke it but his dad heard. He murmured in agreement while looking up a little. Jon was glad his father had come by, but it was time for their visit to end. He needed to get back to work. Blocking things out was the only way he was able to keep going and get up in the morning. It helped that he was so overwhelmed with the abundance of work that had been sent his way.

- Alright mate. I'll see you later.
- Yea okay. Just… make sure you get out a bit. Call your mum. Call Reuben back, too, eh?
- I will.

Jon did his best to keep their conversation short despite the fact that it was evident his father wanted to continue talking and probably come back into the house. That just wasn't going to happen. There was simply far too much that needed to be done. He closed the door after his father and immediately stepped back into the frame of mind he had occupied earlier that morning. His work was waiting, as was his father's silhouette behind the frosted opaque glass door. Apparently his goodbye had been insufficient. It quickly left his mind as he took off his boots and headed back to work. He was glad that he could work from home despite how demanding his job had been of late. As though walking down his hallway backwards in time, he could hear Fiona walking around the house quietly singing to herself. *I've just got a little more work to do, okay darling? I won't be long.*

---

6 - June 16th – Fiona

It happened so quickly that it felt like nothing more than being shoved by commuters on the train for Fiona. Her seatbelt worked flawlessly and kept her firmly rooted to her seat as their car was steered from the road when the tire shredded from the rim of the front driver's-side wheel. Had it been seen from above, the car visibly dipped hard when the tire had disintegrated, Jonathan then overcorrected and sent the vehicle into a quick three-sixty on the road before sliding sideways into the ditch lining the road and making quick and decisive contact with several trees. The car struck the trees driver's-side first and they held their ground against the comparatively flimsy metal frame of the little car. By the time it came to a halt, the body of the car was slightly arced in shape around the frame of the tree that stole and squandered its momentum. Fiona's side remained relatively unscathed but for the glass missing from the window on the back passenger door.

Her head hung loosely over her shoulders and she was slumped in her seat when everything had stopped. She didn't lose consciousness in the event, but sat in shock and her body felt as though it had somehow separated from her. She was unable to move for a while. Various sounds came from the vehicle during the few moments she took to collect herself, for a short time they were all she was capable of comprehending. The repetitive sounds cocooned her for a while where she sat. There was a dripping coming from somewhere; the liquid sounded as though it was dropping onto a hot surface somewhere behind her and quickly evaporating from the heat. The trees creaked above the car as calmly as they had done before it had invaded their domain. They gently clacked against each other and abraded small twigs and bark from each other's limbs as they did so. Fiona murmured to herself under her breath about being cold; something about "don't leave." She reached down for her scarf which still lay stretched out across her legs. When she pulled it there was something preventing its release as Jonathan would without realizing at night with their duvet. ⏐

-    Come on…

She still murmured the words quietly, apparently unaware that she was not in her warm bed that waited empty some twenty miles from where she actually sat. Reaching again for the scarf she felt that it was wet a little further down. She withdrew her hand and wrinkled her face without opening her eyes. Her hair still hung forward, despite it being shorter than she had kept it in a long time, and covered her face slightly. She was uncomfortable and annoyed, as a child would be after being awoken from an exciting dream in a nap on a long car journey.

The touch of the wet fabric of her scarf and the sensation of the wind on her cheeks entering through the driver's side window disturbing her hair grounded her in the reality of her situation. She was not in pain at all. Her neck bothered her slightly and she would later have bruising from where her seatbelt had saved her life, but her skin was not tainted with any new scratches or cuts from the accident. She brushed her hair from her eyes and turned to Jonathan. He lay still in his seat. It was, however, cozily nestled beneath the newly formed convex and bulging interior of the door. His seat had shifted downwards and listed towards the outside of the car. The view from his window, which was now shattered, was obscured by the dark brown bark of the tree. He was pinned into his position. His right leg, closest to the door, was visible for only a few inches lower than his waist, and his left stretched out in front of him as if jarred straight by the steering wheel which had dropped in its place. The open airbag lay like a parachute on his lap.

Slowly, she reached over and shook his shoulder.

-    Darling.

Quietly at first.

-    Jonathan. Jon, baby can you hear me?

With each effort the urgency in her voice became more apparent.

-    Jonathan!

She shook him hard and swore to herself several times in her place while she did her best to free herself from her seatbelt. The clasp, which had clearly saved her life, now stole the brunt of her anger and panic as she scrambled to undo it. After wrestling and swearing for a few seconds she freed herself and moved around onto her knees in the passenger seat. The front of the car was now much more visible, despite the headlights having both gone out. She was unsure at this point if she had passed out at all or how long they had been there, but the slight hint of sunlight far away in the distance suggested that it couldn't have been long. She wailed and shook him again. His eyes were closed and his head seemed to be locked into place with his chin tilted upwards slightly as though he was looking far ahead through closed eyes. She climbed around him, staying careful not to place any of her weight on him should she move him uncomfortably or cause him any pain while trying to help. The door frame had collapsed slightly on Jonathan's side and now held his head in a small cubby space that looked at first glance as though it had been made specifically to house it.

- Okay. Okay. Shit. Okay. Right…

Her voice trembled as she fumbled for her phone in the pocket of her jacket which had been on the back seat and was now on the floor behind her seat. She rang the emergency services, cried down the phone, and waited for what seemed like forever for them to arrive. She lay her scarf over Jonathan and did her best not to move him too much. Whimpering to herself, she nestled closely against him carefully while she quietly waited. She was sure he was breathing.

He was. Faintly. He had a pulse when the ambulance arrived. Fiona rode with him in the back for a journey that seemed remarkably quick given the distance. When the pair of them got to the hospital, Jonathan was taken directly into the ICU and Fiona was ushered into the arms of Jon's parents who had arrived just before them. They looked anxious and scared. The sight of Geoff's face was enough to bring the tears back to Fi's eyes after having stopped in the ambulance thanks to comforting words from the paramedics.

- Bit different to last time, eh?

Geoff smiled a weak grin as he and his wife drew Fiona in for a hug.

- Not now Geoffrey!

His wife snapped at the comment he'd aimed at Fiona. She laughed and sniffed thinking about the last time the three of them had been brought into the hospital for Jonathan's sake. He had slipped down the stairs having been sleepwalking; a habit he'd continued since adolescence according to his family. While he was not injured badly, it had been enough to keep him overnight to see if he'd suffered a concussion in the fall. His parents had visited that evening with Fiona to see if he was alright, and to rub it in that he was brought to hospital wearing only the underpants in which he had fallen, a pair of brown loafers, and a hoodie stained with paint and bleach.

- You look good mate.
- Fuck off dad.

He laughed with his dad and looked down at his fabulous getup.

They had apparently gotten past the *you will not swear at your father* phase that had quite rightly reigned supreme in their house as he grew up.

- Don't speak to your father like that darling. He's only trying to get a reaction out of you.

Jonathan laughed in his hospital bed. He looked tired more than anything. His head ached but no more seriously than it would have had he had a little too much to drink the night before. The only one not laughing in the room was his mum. She eventually caved and remarked that at least the boxers Jonathan had fallen in were not the one's he had worn in university at twenty-one that still had the "ages 12-14" tag in the back.

No. This wasn't like the last time at all. Geoffrey's brief effort to add some comic relief was as far as any smile stretched across any of the three faces waiting silently in the blue-grey waiting area. They watched the newsreel from start to finish enough times that they likely knew it more thoroughly than those involved in each story. Every ten or fifteen minutes the notice of the crash would stretch across the information bar at the bottom of the screen in white letters on a red banner. *...traffic is restricted to one lane after an accident involving one vehicle earlier this evening. The driver is currently in hospital in critical condition while the passenger has been released with only minor injuries. Alcohol or drugs are not believed to have been a factor.*

Each of them circulated back and forth every so often to inquire with the doctors to find out if there was any update on his status. They each took breaks to get coffee and tea several times. At some point, they each forgot briefly why they were there; why they were wide awake inside a windowless room while the sun slowly rose outside at six in the morning. Clara slept briefly on and off in her chair, and would later deny that she had actually been sleeping and that she was instead "resting her eyes." When the doctor finally returned at just before eight the next morning, they looked as if they had all taken the worst red-eye flight imaginable with the bumpiest landing and the most aggressive customs officers with searching fingers. They felt worse than they looked.

-   He responded well initially to the surgery to relieve the pressure on his head.

Fiona exhaled a little, realizing that until then she'd been holding her breath a little unconsciously.

-   However, he has not regained consciousness yet.

Clara, now wide awake after her latest spat of eye-resting interjected:

-   So what does that mean?

- He's in a coma.
- Okay. How long do you think it will be until he wakes up? Will he be alright when he wakes up?

The three of them asked the questions that everyone would expect to ask in such a situation, all knowing that the doctor really couldn't tell them much more than he had already divulged. The final question came from Fiona.

- Is he going to survive?

The doctor paused and sat down slowly.

- Mrs. Eliot-
- Its Platt, I didn't take his name.

The doctor looked blankly as though asking for permission to continue his train of thought, unaffected by her correction.

- Sorry. That's not the point right now…

Clara gently placed her hand on Fi's arm to show that it was fine.

- Since the injuries to Mr. Eliot's – Jonathan's – head were so severe, he is lucky to be alive at the moment. He is still in critical condition. It will be a few days until we know more. I suggest you go home if you need to get some sleep or some clothes in the mean time and we will call you if anything changes for him

Fiona stayed at the hospital for the whole day with Jonathan while his parents went home to sleep and fetch some things for her. She knew she was probably going to have to settle in to the long haul at the hospital. Inside, however, she was screaming for Jonathan to wake up and not leave her alone. It was comforting to be next to him, but even as his machine beeped, she knew she would soon feel just as by herself.

Later in the afternoon, Fiona had settled into the chair she would come to know so well for the next week or so. As she had not been home she was limited to the collection of

34

mindless games on her phone and some books, also on her phone, that she had yet to read. She didn't start one, though. The hospital magazines lent a strange perspective over the situation as they were so out of character for her to even pick them up and thumb through the pages. As a result, she felt even more lost and out of place, suddenly becoming one of the women she saw at the dentist who read such material. She quickly put down the magazine and sat in silence. Despite not wanting to leave Jonathan's side should he wake up alone, she had to use the toilet so she took the opportunity to quickly stretch her legs. *Perhaps he will wake up while I'm gone simply because it's unlucky. I'd take that.* It was the first time that she had been inside a hospital and was actually connected to anything remotely serious. As a child or a teenager she had walked through hospitals as a patient or when visiting friends or family, but only ever for routine procedures or minor ailments. On such occasions she would look casually into each of the rooms she passed and wonder what plagued the poor individual or individuals within. Who had the most serious condition? Who, currently within the walls of the building, would not live to see their next day?

Would Jonathan be the winner of the "most serious condition" competition on this occasion? Was there someone else in the hospital who was losing their battle in a worse way than him? She thrust her hands into her jacket pockets and walked more quickly to the ladies' room.

On her way back she swung by the gift shop as it was on the same floor. Along with an expensive coffee and bagel that she would end up leaving on the counter in Jonathan's room uneaten, she picked up a charger for her phone so that she could call her mum. She had to talk to someone else who was not there.

- Mum, hey.

35

She burst into tears as soon as Kathy answered the call and stared back at her over Skype.

- How are you doing sweetie?

It was a basic question. Obviously they both knew the answer. Fiona had never been fucking worse. All the same, she replied with the response that comes so naturally to everyone who pretends.

- I'm Okay, really.

She sniffed through her words and quickly composed herself so they would be able to talk. They went over the situation and Fiona did her best to explain how everything had happened, how Jonathan was in critical condition, how it had not been anyone's fault, how she was scared.

- Do you need me to come over there to be with you?

Fiona's mum worked for a law firm in Portland, Oregon. It was very early morning for her by the time Fiona had called. She certainly did not expect her mum to make the trip to Scotland.

- No. It's fine. Geoff and Clara have been here a lot, and I'm going to see Alex probably tomorrow as well.

As they talked things over, Fi stared at Jonathan's body laying in the bed beside her rather than at the screen from which her mother's voice came. She recalled the times when he had been in the room out of view of the video-feed after they had slept together during their early relationship when he would have to be silent so as to not call attention to his presence on her mother's end of the call. Kathy loved Jonathan of course, but only eventually. Put shortly, she really didn't know him well until after the two had married; an event to which none had been invited thus causing a ripple effect of pissed-offness throughout both sides of the family. This time the concern was equally shared by mother and daughter with regards to Jonathan's state. *He was actually quieter when he was trying not to be found out by my mum than he's being now.* She laughed a little to herself and remarked at the steady beeping of the machines that were monitoring his vitals. She squeezed his hand with her free hand and returned to the conversation with her mum. Kathy would not be visiting. Jonathan would come around soon and it would turn into the story they would tell at parties and events for the next six decades of their lives.

---

7 - June 21st – Fiona

Reuben had come by twice. He had sat with her for a few hours quietly during his first visit, but they did not have much to talk about. Reuben was Jonathan's friend and she only knew him in passing really. Despite their having lived in the same place now for quite a while, she could not recall a time when Reuben had visited while she had been home, and very rarely when it was just Jonathan. He was a few years older than Jonathan, just a little younger than her. Despite that, he behaved with a nervousness and flailing attitude towards his life that indicated to people watching him that he was much younger. *26 going on 18 this guy…* All the same, it was nice of him to visit. She had no problem with him but just felt much more comfortable when he came by the second time and stayed for just a half hour or so.

- Has he moved or done anything since last time?
- No. He's pretty out of it Reuben.
- Yea. For sure.

She laughed a little to herself and looked up at Reuben who was standing over Jonathan's bed looking confused.

- You aren't very good at this are you.

She smiled while she called him out.

- What do you mean?
- Well. You're looking at him like you either love him passionately or like he's in a museum and you've never seen anything like him before. I kind of hope it's the second one, eh?

He laughed and relaxed a little.

- Yea. I guess I've never really known anyone go through this kind of thing. I don't know what you must be feeling. I really don't want to get in the way or anything eh. Sorry Fi.

His eyes stayed fixed on Jonathan.

- He still looks right though eh.

Fiona laughed again a little bit.

- What do you mean "he looks right?"
- Like, he hasn't been mangled up like some of those car accidents you see on TV when you can't even recognize their faces or they have to get the dental records or something to prove who it was.
- Yea. Most of those people are dead Reuben. Jonathan's still with us.
- Yea. No, you're right.

Reuben had an odd way about him that made everything he did seem strangely apologetic. His stance, the way he carried himself, all the way down to his choice of clothing and his choice of words. The mop of hair he sported was fashioned in the conventional "I haven't changed my look since I was thirteen" style with various tufts and areas poking off into different directions despite the fact that he had to go back to work in the afternoon. Some people were able to pull it off, others actually tried for such a look; Reuben did neither of those things. The face he wore remained confused as he was evidently searching for the right expression to appropriately convey sadness. He looked up at her briefly, forced a half

38

smile, then walked out of the room without saying anything. Despite how little she knew about Reuben, this seemed pretty much par for the course so she went back to reading her magazine and checking her phone periodically while she sat by Jonathan's bed. The world was continuing on as usual. She had received countless emails that needed deleting; people were still dying in the middle east; nothing had changed.

She had only been home once since Jonathan had been in his coma. It was an awful experience for her. It had been as though she was returning home alone forever. Instead she stayed at Tom and Alex's, being sure to take a different road there than the one they had previously tried. Alex had confidently brushed off the situation explaining how lucky Fiona was to have made it out without a scratch and how Jonathan was a tough bastard and would undoubtedly be alright. They had spent the rest of the night drinking wine and talking over her pending PhD thesis until the early hours of the morning while Tom drifted in and out of the conversation. Tom had driven her back to the hospital the following day after just a few hours of sleep and they talked a little in the car. Fiona was pretty sure she would not drive again any time soon.

- Has anyone else come by to see him yet?
- Reuben's been by once. He left me a message saying he'd be by this afternoon, too. Both of Jonathan's parents have been over a lot of course. His mum doesn't say much. Geoff talks a little.
- That's good then. I've been meaning to go by but I can't really do it yet. It's not that I don't want to.
- Tom it's fine. Everyone deals with shit like this totally differently.

They both relaxed in the car a little more and he evidently felt more comfortable having explained himself. She looked out of the window at the sky on the drive back to the hospital. Having been inside so much for the past week she had forgotten how beautiful the sky in Scotland could be. "Scotland really knows how to do the sky, eh?" It was a statement Jonathan had made so often during their time there. He was not wrong. There was something about the sky in Scotland that was unlike anywhere else either of them had seen. Her gaze beyond the glass remained constant until they pulled into the parking lot of the hospital and he let her out.

- I'd say I'll come in next time but there won't be one I'm sure. He's going to wake up before I visit and then he'll have something to be pissed at me for.

Fiona laughed and thanked him for the ride. She felt better and walked across the lot with slightly more pep in her step than she had experienced for what seemed like an interminably long time.

After Reuben had left in the afternoon she woke up beside Jonathan's bed. She had apparently fallen asleep in her chair after talking again with her mum on Skype. Her hand was rested atop Jonathan's while he lay motionless in his bed. She had been unconsciously moving her thumb up and down the back of his hand in her sleep as she had done in the car when they had crashed. His hand was warm from her touch. It was the evening of the fifth day now. She had not thought about the time that had passed since their accident. To her it could have been minutes, hours, or years. For that reason, she had not thought about the possibility that things may have changed in terms of what their approach could be to draw him out of his coma. She was aware, however, that the doctor had explained some time ago that the longer he stayed in his coma,

40

the more likely it would be that they would have to intervene with another surgery to relieve the pressure on Jonathan's brain otherwise he would be more susceptible to brain damage. Staring into space and thinking about nothing in particular, she continued to gently caress his hand while he slept.

---

8 - June 22nd – Fiona

Jonathan died at just after one-thirty that afternoon. After having been called in for surgery to relieve the pressure in his head, his heart stopped while in the OR and the doctors could not resuscitate him. Fiona sat quietly next to Jonathan's empty hospital bed after being told the news until she realized the sun had gone down and she was sat alone in darkness. For the first time in her adult life she felt completely alone, with no way of knowing what to do next. She thought about the medical dramas she used to watch during her university degree when she was supposed to be studying. This part was never shown. After the patient died, the ominous or morose musical tones would rise and the scene would shift to something else – usually credits. There was no music for her; no shift to another scene. She just sat alone; she waited for something else to happen to her; for the credits to roll. Eventually her body could no longer play the game that her mind so wished it could. She was cold and hungry and tired. She needed to use the bathroom. Various responsibilities began flooding into her head like a tidal wave of insurmountable pressure until she could hear her heartbeat resound like a speaker with the bass turned up to eleven against the grey-blue hospital walls. The heavy throbbing sound emanating from her was real; more real than the beeping of the machine that had kept Jonathan with her for a week longer could have ever been.

She quickly gathered her things and left the room without turning around to look back. A memory she would never choose to revisit but that would revisit her against her will for years to come would be the last room in which she saw her husband alive. Her movements were clumsy and she dropped things in her haste but collected them with ease. The rubber soles of her summer flats squeaked quietly against the linoleum floor of the hospital building. When she reached the parking lot where Alex was waiting for her, she took a large, shaky breath in and felt the weight of the air itself crush her chest from the inside as she stepped into Alex's car. When she exhaled it was a noise that sounded undoubtedly like pain.

---

9 - August 30th – Jonathan

Drinks with Reuben were seldom calm. His demeanour was fantastic to Jon at the best of times, so after a few drinks he became even more entertaining. The same could not be said for Jon's own countenance of late and he knew that but offered no apology. He was sure Reuben expected none.
- It's really fucking good to see you man.
- Yep. It's good for sure.
Tom was due to join them later. Alex was working on her PhD thesis. She had apparently been taking things just as hard as Jon. He let the thought slip from his mind with a large mouthful of Guinness as he looked down the bar while Reuben was talking. The place they had gone was new. That was good. It still smelled vaguely of renovations and wood shavings with a hint of a latex paint lingering in the air.

Several long nights of punters drinking and spilling beer would, of course, eradicate that new smell and take over so that the aroma suited the environment. There were plenty of other groups at the bar, mostly students and young professionals from the looks of things. It was a slightly pricier beer thanks to the atmosphere but there was a great deal of money floating around in student pockets in any university town, especially given the time of year. Students were just beginning to cash their loan checks before classes began in a week or so, soon the overseas ones would arrive and such places would be heaving every night of the week. Come December, though, the funds would dwindle and hands would clasp the half pints or bottles of the cheapest beer rather than the presently popular dual-wielding of pints.

Yes. It was good in there. Several of the groups who had already begun their night leant on the rough edge of the natural wood bar. It looked as though it had been cut from one large tree and left unfinished on purpose as it hung over the natural stone by which people stood. The ceiling was low with wood beams and the walls alternated between natural stone and exposed brick. It was evidently an old building that had been brought to life with some serious money. Jon hoped it would do well as he took a second large drag from his pint.

- What on earth are you drinking anyway mate?
- I'm not sure actually. They've got all of these local brews. I just got one that sounded cool. Something with velvet in the name. It's decent though.

Jon tried a swig of it and agreed.

- Tom'll like it here. He knows his beer for sure.

It was true. Without being an anorak about it, Tom had developed a sound understanding of so many different beers. It had been his pastime with his dad for the years until he had died. Tom had apparently continued the tradition himself

43

much to Alex's chagrin at their house. Had Jon and Fiona made it to Alex and Tom's kitchen some months ago they would have been given the tour of different beer bottles lining the tops of the kitchen cupboards that Tom had most recently been working on. Jon had yet to go back to their house. He was fairly sure he never would.

- I'm not joking, I came to a place like this about this time last year, must have been just after the students started, and some bloke came in, a midget, dressed like a Smurf, handcuffed to another guy. The other guy was normal height. Pretty tall actually.
- What on earth are you talking about mate?

Reuben was on a rant that was unaffected by whether or not people were listening to it. Jon had experienced many before so he was not particularly shocked by the statement.

- He was painted blue and everything. Had a little white hat on. He wasn't like annoyed, though. It must have been some prank or dare or something. He looked like he was having a great time.
- Yea. That's Scotland for you I guess.

Jon continued his beer. It was really hitting the right spot. The pain in his back from the accident was dull but present and the beer seemed to work as a tailored elixir for his discomfort. He laughed a little at Reuben's odd story. His stiffened wrists began to slowly loosen from the repetitive pint lift and the comfortable place that the other had found to rest on the bar.

Earlier in the day he had worked out at home and his body hurt for it. Since Fiona, he had left things alone in his little weight room to gather dust while he felt his muscles seemingly do the same. It was something he had shared with Fiona. They were both in good shape for their age and they did their best to keep it that way. Because he sat down all day for work when he was not giving presentations, he felt the pressure even more so than he used to. His back ached intolerably now when he stretched. His progress had been stunted and withdrawn by the long term effects of the accident. He knew he was lucky to be alive after what had happened and even luckier to be able to walk and live relatively unimpeded, but it was still total shit that he was in such worse shape than just a few months earlier. He cracked his knuckles in between stints of resting against the bar. He felt irritable. There was no comfortable position in which he could carry himself. Either the inch-wide gash in his back stretched like dry lips in the wind and rubbed against his shirt, his wrists burned causing his fingers to go numb after resting against the bar for too long, or he leant sideways with one elbow against the bar and caused his neck to ache without respite after only seconds. *This is total horseshit.*

After getting frustrated for a few seconds longer, he stopped himself from complaining, even if it was only internal. As far as Reuben was concerned, he was totally fine. All else aside, he had lived; Fiona had not.

Tom arrived about an hour after the two had been standing. When he did, they moved to one of the barrels-turned-tables about ten feet from the bar and each ordered another drink. Jon was reminded of his university days when he would finger through the coins in his pocket to ensure that he had enough for another pint before 10pm before eventually placing countless beers absentmindedly on his visa card by one in the morning. It would be unwise to do that this time.

-    How are you doing mate?
The default response was queued in both Jon and Reuben and one of them was probably even telling the truth.

-    Yea good.

45

-       Aye not bad at all mate.

It was clear from Tom's attitude that he, too, did not want to talk about the elephant in the room. It was the first time that Jon had been out for a beer in quite a while. They were content to talk about all the things that would have come up had Jon and Fiona made it to their house a few months earlier. Elephants like this one were like a cancer; they were either impossible to avoid or completely unspoken of. Once it began, the conversation could only be about that. Jon recalled the memory of a student in his high school who had been diagnosed with some kind of cancer a few years before graduation. He could not even remember the kid's name, just that he had cancer. It was clear that Alex had been taking things hard and this was a break for Tom. Reuben repeated his story about the midget-Smurf he had seen the previous year to Tom and got the same muted response; this by no means slowed him down and he continued to talk throughout the evening providing a much needed white noise machine that kept Jon's various demons at bay.

After a few more drinks, the various bullshit façades had lifted and the three men could talk more candidly. Despite being the oldest of the three, it had been well established in most of his circles of friends that Reuben had not acted his age since he was ten. Since then, he had cultivated an excellent balance of extreme immaturity coupled with the occasional statement steeped in so much logic and well-reasoned good sense that it was alarming to think he was not more successful than he was.

Reuben Crowell was twenty-six and lived four doors up from the house in which he had been raised as a child. His mum still lived there, while his dad had moved down to London several years earlier to be with a woman ten years his senior. This was a move that Reuben failed both to understand or support so he had never actually been down to visit despite being on otherwise good terms with his old man. At twenty-one he had just graduated from a journalism program with mediocre grades and the dream of becoming an author. After having been rejected by every publisher who had laid eyes on his work he seemed to be granted some sort of pity and offered a job as an editor with one of the smaller publishing firms. Since then he'd worked his way up, proved that he was not as spaced out or offbeat as his un-brushed hair suggested, and eventually started his own small publishing firm in Edinburgh. This had failed spectacularly by the time he was twenty-four, but the contacts he had gathered had ensured that he would be looked after in the industry until he really cocked things up – a situation everyone saw as eventually inevitable. Jon had met Reuben at a university function about six months before he had started seeing Fiona through friends he could no longer remember. The student-professor-academic life was awfully transient for most.

Despite his success and his abundance of confidence that miraculously formed after a few beers, he remained single and had settled into this role comfortably. He was good at his job and invested all of his time into it leaving very little else beyond his circle of friends. Jon watched him talk while they were drinking and thought quietly of his approval towards this trait in his friend. It had worked for Reuben.

- Anyway guys. My sister's wedding next month, want to swing by and have some drinks?
- Don't your parents already think you've got a boyfriend Roob? If you bring two of us it's going to look pretty open and shut mate.

Tom laughed at his own joke and continued on with his beer. Both he and Jon knew Reuben's sister but hardly well enough to attend her wedding.

- Don't be a twat. Not the bit in the church, idiot. Just the bit afterwards.
- The reception?
- What does that mean?
- Roob. You're 26, you know what the reception means.

It was ridiculous to watch the look of confusion in his face. They saw quickly that he did, in fact, not know what the reception meant.

- The reception is the drinks and dinner afterwards mate. It's usually at like a hotel or something.

Tom cleared it up quickly for Reuben and then headed over to the bar to order another round for the three of them. He knew more about the beer than either Jon or Reuben would so it was best to just let him do his thing.

- Ok. Yea. I think it's that.
- Why don't you bring a date though, Roob?

Tom and Reuben then jumped into a long conversation about why Reuben was still single. Jon knew how it would end so he turned his attention back to the room which was now starting to fill up more as the evening drew on.

They eventually reached the understanding that Reuben's sister's future husband was from elsewhere and had very few male friends that he was bringing to the wedding, so there were seats to fill. Apparently Reuben's mother had also been confident of the fact that he would not be bringing a girlfriend so it had been her idea to ask Tom and Jon if they would like to attend. Tom accepted the offer after ensuring that Alex would be allowed to go before quickly realizing that she still probably wouldn't want to by then. His glance immediately shifted to Jon to see how he would react. Astonishingly, they had made it so far into the evening without being overwhelmed by the sadness that seemed to seep from Jon's pores everywhere he went, but it was eventually too late.

- Don't feel obliged mate. I know it's still way too fucking soon.
- No it's fine.
- I shouldn't have brought it up man, forget about it eh?

Fucking pity is so much worse. Don't turn into some pitying prick now Roob.

- I said it's fine mate.

There was a little more mustard in his tone the second time. Both Tom and Reuben felt it quickly.

- Aye, good. Yea. It's like the third week of September. I wrote it down somewhere but I can't remember what it was.
- Of course you did. Well done mate.

Jon remained out of it for the rest of the evening. He wanted to get back to work. Fiona's singing was probably still echoing through his house and he was not there to listen to it. The beer tasted sour in his mouth and he nursed the one he was on for the rest of the evening without saying anything about it. All the people in the bar enjoying their evening quickly made him angry. Apparently his rage had kept itself quietly hidden a few steps back from his face because his friends seemed not to notice and continued their night with Reuben dominating the conversation as per the usual.

---

10 - September 12th – Jonathan

This was good news.

- Okay. I understand. Thankyou sir.

He hung up the phone and tossed it onto his desk amidst a pile of papers. Work was going well. It kept him occupied under the circumstances. Breathing out slowly with his hands up behind his head he swivelled back and forth in his chair. He leant back and looked up at the ceiling; it would need painting soon; he would do it when he was not so busy. *Fuck. When's Roob's sister's thing...* With everything seemingly taking flight with his job, he had been so busy that he was worried he had missed it. *He'd have called.* Jon stretched forwards again and set his eyes back on his phone to text Reuben for the actual details as he was sure he was never given them properly. After a quick text – responded to almost instantaneously by Reuben – he had figured out that it was on the twenty-first. He got the time and the place, what he was meant to wear, and an inexplicable picture of a dog fucking another dog. Reuben was a twelve-year-old most days.

Jon got up and walked back to the bedroom – work could wait a little while he explored his options for this wedding reception. He had texted Tom earlier in the week to make sure that it really was a reception after it was clear that Reuben was pretty dense about the whole subject. Neither he nor Tom wanted to arrive in a tux to a pub or in jeans to some fancy hotel ballroom. It was in a hotel conference centre as both of them had initially thought, but it was not due to be black-tie – just formal. The double closet in their bedroom had previously consisted of eighty-percent Fiona's gear and twenty-percent Jon's. He had a few options so far. He looked sideways at the full-length mirror which stood adjacent to the closet. Some of Fiona's smaller articles of clothing still clung to its corners. He passed a palm absent-mindedly across his chin and through his beard. Apparently he had let things go for a few weeks. Still shirtless as it was early in the morning, he turned as much as his neck would allow so he could see the scar down his back with a better view. While not fully healed, it was well on its way to becoming just another tattoo of experience. He arched his arm over his shoulder and ran his fingers over the uneven scar tissue while regarding it carefully in the reflection of the mirror. Jon wondered how it may have felt for Fiona's fingers to have explored this new topography of his body. It was wide at its worst. Towards his lower back were the shard-sized fleck scars dotted around sporadically which were fully healed. As he traced further down with his eyes, the scar eventually reached its end and disappeared. After a few minutes of observing himself quietly, he turned around to properly face himself and relieve the strain in his neck from having turned his head for too long. So much of him was not the same.

When they had got married, he had probably been twenty pounds heavier. He knew he looked thin as he stared at himself in the mirror remembering their speed-style wedding. They had certainly taken some flack for doing it on the fly and not making it a big deal, but neither had been concerned with the institution as a whole. Jon's mum had been the most upset, which had in turn pissed Fiona off that her mum was not more upset about it. *People react so damn weirdly to things.*

- I think I'm in love with you.

That was how he had managed to get the words out the first time during their trip to Spain. *Of course she didn't say it back right away. Of all the ways to tell someone you feel… "I think…" She definitely deserved better than that.* It had not taken her long to catch up with him, though. Their trip to Spain was just a flurry of memories in Jon's head even weeks after they had got home. Unplanned and unorganized, it had turned into three of the best days of his short life. He knew she had enjoyed it too, despite the fact that it had evidently scared the shit out of her to just leave for Spain from Scotland on a whim. That was something that much older people were able to do; people with more money and comparatively more time than they had.

After a few minutes of quiet remembering, Jon was back in their bedroom standing alone staring past his own reflection. *This is going to have to be a real fucking performance.* He dreaded the reception he had agreed to attend. It just seemed way too soon to be heading out to do things like this. He felt bad for having gone to the pub with Tom and Roob already. How long were you meant to keep the brakes on for? What was an appropriate amount of time to be seen having fun? People always made comments about how sad he looked or how he should be getting out of the house but it was not far from his mind that in the past he had been a part of conversation responsible for judging some poor lady at the university whose husband had died for being out with her friends just a month or so later. *What the hell was she supposed to do, though?* Was she happy because she was out? Was it better than being at home? People couldn't possibly understand how to deal with it until it happened to them.

It didn't take long for Jon to realize to himself that his internal questioning was ultimately moot. He did not want to go. It had nothing to do with what others thought of his behaviour, it just sounded like a difficult evening of forced socialization. If Fiona had joined him, it would have been a team effort. She would undoubtedly stay home this time when he walked out of the door with Reuben. He would surely hear her singing and padding about semi-quietly while he forced down a beer that he didn't want.

11- June 30th – Fiona

The numbness was starting to wane, if not excruciatingly slowly. Sweatpants and long sweaters had been Fiona's staple wardrobe since Jonathan's funeral a few days earlier. It was hot outside but she didn't notice. Her days consisted of the same routine. After spending another night at Alex and Tom's after everything had happened she had gone home to her empty apartment. Of all the things that terrified her in her state, she relaxed in the knowledge that she simply would not clean the place just yet. Everything still smelled of Jonathan. It smelled of both of them. She wondered if she no longer smelled the same now that there was no longer a "both of them." *Am I a single person now? Am I a widow?* It sounded awfully odd in her mind. She would wake up early every day at about five o'clock. This, unfortunately, was usually after only three or four hours of sleep, but that didn't seem to matter. While she crept around the house in the morning, she was careful to stay as quiet as she could lest she wake Jonathan up. She would slide from the bed with extreme caution and let the door close almost the whole way before placing her palm against it while holding the handle down to prevent a snap of the latch as it closed completely.

Her footsteps on the carpet were noiseless, as were her practiced padded steps on the laminate kitchen floor as she prepared her morning cup of tea. She knew the kettle boiling would not wake Jonathan as he seemed to be able to sleep through that every morning; just the sound of someone moving around made him stir. She had laundry to do later, still from before their accident. Looking down the hall she recalled the first time Jonathan had convinced her to go over to his house. They had been spending time together around the university for a while, but neither seemed to be sure what was really going on between them. Fi had been skeptical of the notion of starting a new relationship as she was so far from her home in the US. The American twang in her accent was still very much intact. It must have been in the winter because it was awfully cold outside when she had been deciding whether or not to go to his house.

- Don't worry. I'll come and pick you up so you won't have to walk.

He had sounded so nonchalant about it. He seemed to love her already despite his tone and it had scared the shit out of her.

- Ok, but I'm going to need a cup of tea when I get there.
- Yea that's fine.

Jonathan had driven the short way over to her apartment to pick her up late in the evening. She was still getting used to the cold so he knew she'd be feeling it more than he would be. Their drive back to his apartment was short but he had spent the journey over there evidently doing his best to warm up the car as much as possible. The fans were on full blast for heat while he sat, clearly too warm, in a t-shirt and jeans as she had scurried across the lawn and into the passenger seat. It immediately felt cozy and warm. When they got back to his house he had the kettle boiled and began steeping the tea while Fiona took off her boots.

- Wait here just a sec'
- Okay.

She was uncomfortable being in his house, but set herself to work on making the tea while he was out of the room. She silently questioned where he might have shot off to just as they had arrived home. A dull humming that had been coming from a room just around the corner from the kitchen ceased, a door clicked shut, and she heard him heading her way.

- This should warm you up a little if we watch a film or something eh?

He was holding a sweater and a pair of thick woollen socks that he had been warming in the dryer since she had agreed to come over.

Fiona continued to creep around the house at just after five in the morning. She had a few hours before the reality of the situation would set in again; when Jonathan would not wake up in the room down the hall; when they would not read together in the morning before each had to go to work. She looked out at the sky through the kitchen window and watched the tops of the trees swaying in the wind; it was strong. The leaves blew in flurries and gusts while still clinging to each limb with valiant effort. Everything beyond the glass was doused in a red-orange hue from the morning sun just beginning to assert its dominance over the clouds in the distance. Maintaining her silent gait, she grabbed her phone from where it was plugged in by her bedside and took it back to the living room so she could talk again with her mum. She repeated her silent method of opening and closing each door on the way there so she would be able to speak without worrying of the consequences.

- Hey mum, how are you doing?
- Why are you whispering I can't hear you?

Just like that, the illusion was shattered. *I can't just be honest with her and say that I don't want to wake Jonathan up.*

- Sorry. Must be a bad connection, I'll ring you back.
- No it seems to be fine now. How are you doing baby girl?

Her mum spoke to her with a tone that suggested she may have still been a young child. Sometimes it worked. This time it was scratching and unpleasant with every word.

They talked for an hour or so. By the time they hung up, the red hue had left the sky and the day was underway for everyone else. Fiona had to face the fact that, once again, Jonathan was not about to get up and stumble to the kitchen before getting ready for work. Thinking about it slowly, she wondered how this would work for the rest of her life. Whenever she had left or been left by a previous boyfriend it was the norm to refer to him as an ex. She would always refer to Jonathan as her husband. People would be sure she was still married. Jonathan *was* her husband, but Jonathan also *had been* her husband. In any case, he was an indivisible part of her. *'Widow' really was an awful word.* Breathing out slowly she wondered what to do. Geoff had already called the university on her behalf so she wouldn't have to call in to work until she was ready. They would miss her, but they would survive just fine. This was just it, though. There was nothing to drive her forwards. Fiona still expected to meet Jon from work, or to pick him up from the airport from a trip, or to hear him arguing on the phone in his office. Being idle wasn't something she was used to.

Crying had become a staple part of her day. As contrary as it was to her, the act of it no longer bothered her. It became just another function that her body worked through on a day to day basis. She showered, brushed her teeth, did laundry, and moved around the house silently while maintaining streams from each eye and a perpetual look of vacancy. *FUCK.* The doorbell rang with Alex standing on the other side of the frosted glass window. With everything that she had not been doing, Fiona had forgotten once more that plans made in the past eventually became the present and she was required to do things. *Shit.*

-   Hang on, one sec.

She called over to the door to buy some time without really knowing why. She stood rooted in her spot and bit the nail of her right ring finger anxiously. Her sweatpants getup became apparent quickly as she regarded herself looking down.

- Sorry about that.

Fiona opened the door and let Alex in without too many words. It was simpler to just be quiet at this point.

- Hey. We have stuff to do. You look like crap darling. What the hell?
- Yea sorry I forgot you were coming.
- I figured. But yea, get ready.

Alex's no-nonsense approach had the effect of kicking Fiona into gear. She turned to get ready while Alex waited in the kitchen without removing her jacket. She evidently meant business and had things to do. Alex continued to call down the hallway with a list of the tasks that the two were going to get done during the day while she was still texting or emailing or something or other on her phone in the kitchen. For someone who really was not all that busy, she gave off the impression that she ran a multi-national and multi-million-dollar corporation from her phone.

- Okay. I didn't hear any of the shit we have to do. Let's just go.
- Yea. Sounds good.

They drove quietly and milled around town on the various important errands that Alex had worked out. The radio continued spewing the latest on the various attacks and bombings overseas. Fiona was ambivalent towards each of the stories. She wondered, though, if she would have felt differently about Jonathan's death had it been at the hands of another. Would she have felt differently if he had died among a group? *Would I be allowed to be so sad? Is anyone allowed to be?* After looking out of the window for several minutes musing over her morose subject matter while Alex and the radio battled it out for who was loudest and more persistent, Fiona realised that she did not even know how to feel as it was that Jonathan was gone. He did not feel gone, but still she felt alone.

- What's going on with work for you at the moment anyway Fi?
- Hmm?
- Like, you're obviously not going back for a while at least, but did you sort it all out?
- Geoff already did.

Fiona had first met Alex at work. There was a small special collections department at the university library that required only one full-time member of staff: that was Fiona. She had started working there with the goal of saving some money up before taking on graduate studies in a few years. After moving up from shelving books along with eighteen-year-old students, she had proved that she knew what she was doing and actually had a certain level of respect for the books that most did not possess. Fiona had a small room in the basement of the library with one glass wall, and about twenty sets of high shelves full of periodicals, journals, and a strange collection of more specific and less-requested editions of texts that most of the students had neither heard of nor knew actually existed. Students were granted permission to use any of the special collections material in that room. In it were several desk-cubicles, some long tables with leather chairs, and various equipment for handling some of the more valuable pieces.

Most of the students who frequented the special collections room were from the department of theology or divinity, some English literature students also showed up, and the occasional med student showed up for older editions of better known texts. Alex had no use for the special collections room. This was apparent to Fiona on her first visit. As in an old bookshop on a London back street, Fiona would emerge from between the shelves at each visitor and assist the customer in finding the obscurity they sought. Alex had not needed such help. She arrived with the noise from her headphones clearly audible to everyone in the room – which had only been Fiona – and her laptop open in her arms with the power cord trailing on the floor behind her. She had scanned the room quickly, placed her laptop down on the nearest long table – loudly – and started to unpack her things to post up and presumably do some work under the deafening tones of whatever noise she was listening to. Fiona emerged quickly from amongst a small section of literary periodicals from the 1919-1922 and approached her new guest to see what she needed.

- No I'm alright thanks love, just here to get some studying done. It's too busy upstairs.
- Oh... Okay. Cool.

Alex had taken Fiona by surprise with her confidence. Special Collections was not meant to function as the rest of the library did. Students were only really meant to use the space for specific research purposes as it was such a small department. Fiona mulled this over in her head while standing a few yards away from her intruder. After looking around and seeing that they were the only two in the room, she had decided to simply let it go and leave Alex to study. Six hours later the girl was still there. Her music still blared from her headphones. *How is this girl not deaf yet... Maybe she is. Maybe that's why she has to listen to it so loud.*

- Excuse me.
- Yea what's up?

Alex pulled the headphones from her ears and tucked her long blonde hair behind her ears. She looked up at Fiona from her chair with an endearing stare.

- Well, this department is only open until 5:30.
- Yea for sure.
- Well, it's 6:10. I've got to close up and go home.

On their first meeting, Fiona had assumed that this girl was a few years her senior. It turned out that this girl was, at that time, just twenty-two when Fi was twenty-five, she had just been extremely confident in herself apparently.

- Oh. Sorry love I'll get myself together here.
- No rush. It's just me anyway, just wanted to let you know!

Following that, Alex had felt bad for keeping Fiona after hours and took her for a beer to make up for it. They had been close friends since then and Tom had gotten along well with Jonathan.

It occurred to Fiona in the car that this was the first time Alex had known her while she was not with Jonathan. She was immediately concerned that it would change the nature of their friendship or ruin things in some way. Her heart beat a little faster in her chest while she looked out of the car window before she controlled herself and tried to relax a little more. There was just far too much to be concerned about at this point for her to begin creating more problems in her head. Besides, that had always been Jonathan's area of expertise rather than hers. She looked across at Alex in the driver's seat as they were finishing their rounds.

- You were such a bitch that day.
- What day!
- In Special Collections. Just walking in like you owned the place.

They laughed together as they drove on to meet Tom after he'd finished work.

- Thanks for bringing me out today Alex. ∕

---

12 - September 21ˢᵗ – Jonathan

- You got any beer in the fridge mate?

Reuben called loudly and obnoxiously from the living room to Jon. Jon was getting ready in his bedroom while Reuben waited with his feet on the table – shoes still on – down the hall.

- Should be mate, get up and get it yourself.

They bantered a while, each yelling back and forth down the hall before Reuben eventually caved and hauled himself off the couch to get a drink. He brought two opened beers to Jon's door passed one to his friend. Contrary to the usual, Reuben had put some serious effort into his look: black suit, light pink shirt, clean black lace-ups and silver cufflinks. He looked as professional and put together as he probably could do without having brushed his hair or tended to his mess of stubble. It was still a mystery to everyone whether he could actually grow a proper beard or not. Reuben sipped his beer and regarded his friend who was struggling with the decision of whether or to wear a tie.

- Put the tie back dumbass.
- I like the tie.

Reuben quickly snatched the tie away and threw at across the room so that it joined a large pile of unwashed clothes on Jon's floor.

- Good to see you're keeping things together mate.

- Yea. Been busy. I'll get around to it before I really need to.

His voice suggested that he was really trying to be ok with things. It came through a little bit, but the lines in his face had deepened with the weight he had lost and the weight he'd gained. *We're going to be way too early to this thing.*

- Does Toni know that Tom and I are coming?
- Yea she's fine with it. Mum wants to see you guys as well.
- Yea.

Jon concentrated on his cufflinks in between sips of beer. The two tasks went poorly together.

- Is Tom bringing Alex?
- I asked him today but he never got back to me. Last I heard she wasn't coming. I think she's doing better, though.

They looked at each other while sipping beer. As Reuben finished swallowing his mouthful he added:

- I didn't mean, like, better than you; or that it's like a competition. I just meant-
- I know dude, calm yourself.

Jon threw the tie at Reuben before finishing his bottle, taking a large handful of painkillers with the final swig, and heading off to the kitchen in search of another beer. *Got to delay this shit as much as possible.* Jon, along with everyone else, knew that Roob's mum was prone to some wonderfully personal questions. At a time when beer was just beer and things could be laughed at this was bad enough, but the thought of hearing Fiona's name whispered around him quietly before being thrust into full-fledged conversations about it with her was too much to comprehend. *Don't be a tosser. Nobody is going to ask or say anything. It's Toni and Dave's day. I'm background noise. I'll fill space at the bar.* He grabbed another beer before Reuben could usher the two of them out to head down to the venue.

The patio doors at the reception remained open throughout the evening. Jon spent most of his time looking out over the adjacent golf course and neighbouring houses as the sun was going down. The wind on his face was the same wind that had brought him back to life in the upturned driver's seat of his car not two months ago. He sipped a drink and leant against the railing, ignoring the hint of a bite that the wind possessed in the late evening. People were happy around him. He was not upset. He watched different groups associating with one another, family members colliding from both sides of the newly conjoined family, and children running around with exhausted parents observing from their tables. Jon felt nothing. *I should be working.* Fiona was there. She was singing at home, walking around in her little t-shirt, coffee in one hand and usually a book in the other. This time last year they had just got married.

- We have to go see your dad soon darling.
- I know, I think he's the only one that seems really happy about how it all happened.

Jon was right. Most of their friends had been annoyed that they hadn't received an invitation to their wedding. Geoffrey seemed to be the only one who understood that if everyone was in the same boat, nobody had the right to feel offended or targeted. Jon and Fi had hated the idea of marriage at all anyway.

- So what should *newlyweds* be doing this soon after their wedding then babe?

Fiona was leaning against the doorframe of Jon's office while he worked. Looking up, he saw her standing and waiting for

63

him, of course with her coffee and her book, in her little t-shirt
— only her little t-shirt.

- Well that's not fair, is it darling?

She laughed a little and came to sit on his lap, being careful
not to spill her coffee on her bare skin in the process. He
pursed his lips as though trying to reach her coffee without his
hands so she lifted the mug and he took a large drag.

- Hey are you going to leave me any of it at all?!
- Well. I was trying to make sure we finished it quickly
  actually.

Fi got the message and quickly put her coffee down. She
dropped her book on the ground and wrapped her legs around
Jon's waist as he stood up slowly with her in his arms. Her
book lay discarded on the ground, the page lost and the pages
crumpled under the weight of the hard-cover while the spine
stared up at the ceiling. Jon pressed his fingers into each of
her thighs while she kissed his neck. He walked them quickly
to their bedroom and left the door wide open before throwing
her down on the unmade bed that they had only an hour ago
vacated.

Sex with the sun streaming in was so much better than
sex in the dark. Something about the fact that it was
happening while everyone else was either at work or doing
something productive just made it so much better. Jon pushed
Fiona against the bed roughly. She fought back and bit her lip
making quiet squeaks of approval while staring into his eyes in
feigned anger or fear. As Fiona had very little to remove she
quickly caught Jon up and ensured that his skin found its
rightful place against hers. She bit his shoulder, gently at first,
before sinking her teeth in firmly as he went to work. A flurry
of already dishevelled sheets and blankets swept each side table
clean and exhausted them both.

-   That's probably what most newlyweds would be doing, right?
-   Yea. But I think we do it better than 'most.'

They laughed and laid exhausted on the bed amidst the hurricane they had created. Fiona's t-shirt was now around one arm and she lay with one leg over Jon's and rested her head against his chest. She readjusted and placed her t-shirt between her legs while they both breathed heavily.

-   I love you.

Jon mumbled in agreement before adding his own sentiments.

-   Still scared?
-   Of course, but it's a good kind of scared.

He would take it. That was a much better answer than he had got in the past. As the warmth from their activities began to wane as they lay beside each other, Fiona got up slowly, kissed Jon on the chest, and walked down the hallway to retrieve her now stone cold coffee from his office. He watched her arse as she padded down the hall and groaned as he sat up to once again face the day ahead of him.

Jon thought about Fiona at home while he leant over the railing at the reception and readied himself to go back inside and pretend to be sociable thanks to the wind and the cigarette smoke.

-   Jon!

Sounds like Roob. Sounds drunk. Could be worse. Could be his mum. He turned to where the voice was coming from and saw Reuben, hair actually organized for once, heading towards him in the company of a short blond woman that he did not recognize.

-   Roob. How's it going mate?
-   Aye it's alright mate. This is Karen.
-   Very nice to meet you, I hope he's behaving himself.

Jon gestured towards Reuben while making his joke. The woman seemed a little confused at the comment and he felt the need to backtrack.

- So how do you know Toni and Dave, Karen?
- I actually don't! I've only met Toni once or twice through Reuben.

Now it was Jon's turn to be confused. He had assumed that this girl had stumbled onto Reuben's arm at some point over the course of the evening. It turned out, however, that they had met before. *Has he mentioned her? Have I just totally forgotten? Am I a huge asshole who just doesn't listen? How is it possible that Roob has some woman in his life and I have no goddamn idea about it?*

- Oh I see. How long have you known Reuben then?

She thought about it a little while Jon did his best to tell his own face to mask his confusion.

- I guess its just about two months now.

The three made pleasant conversation for a little while. Jon continued his barrage of internal self-questioning about the whole situation. In reality it really was a non-situation. Reuben was polite, well put together, reserved in conversation until called upon, and respectful of his 'girlfriend.' *Maybe that's what's throwing me. He's never like this.*

After a sufficiently polite amount of time and champagne in a conversation he had not expected, Jon made the excuse to leave briefly. He walked briskly to the bathroom and heard several mumblings from groups he passed with one distinctively clear word: Fiona. His heart was beating more quickly again. The dripping noise of the engine on its back and the sounds of mechanical pain echoed dully in his ears as he picked up his pace and eventually made it across the hall to the men's room. Lifting each arm and peering inside his jacket he acknowledged that, despite the cold, he had begun sweating through his shirt. Past the point of safe-return, he had to keep his jacket on to hide his perspiration and discomfort, thus making it worse as the night drew on. *Fuck*. The world had very much continued since Fiona had died. He stared at himself in the mirror and splashed some cold water over his face. He looked older. The lines in his face suggested that much longer than two months had passed since he had cared to notice. His suit hung off him thanks to his weight loss since Fiona had gone. He had to get home. She would be waiting; padding around the house in her t-shirt humming some song that he didn't know.

Jon's panic attack in the bathroom would not be drawn out. He would not be allowed to stare worriedly at his face any longer without drawing unwanted questions as the sound of the door quickly made it to his ears. He quickly grasped at some paper towels from the dispenser and carefully dabbed his face. Two men came in at the same time and marched to the urinals, each with a pint glass in hand. Jon checked his watch to find that it was almost eleven. Despite their evident intoxication, both men deftly placed their pints atop their urinals being careful not to let any surface touch the rim of each glass – this was apparently a ritual that had been performed many times before this one.

- Yea, he looks better than I thought he would.
- I'm surprised he's even here to be honest. It's still pretty soon.

I'm literally standing ten fucking feet from you. Did they not recognize Jon? Had enough time passed that they no longer knew his face. He checked his own face in the mirror to see if he did, indeed, recognize himself. Jon quickly realized that he did not recognise the faces of either of the beer-balancers. However, that mattered not. They could only have been talking about he and Fiona. What else was there to mention in such a way? What else could they possibly have felt the

67

need to wait until the privacy of the men's room to bring up? He was sure.

Jon swiftly turned and left the reflection that had been staring back at him angrily. He left the beer-balancers to continue their discussion of his life not ten feet from him. It was time to go home. The sweat marks beneath his armpits had grown substantially in the time he was in the bathroom. He looked at his watch again. It was five to twelve. His wrists quickly realised their pain as they had apparently been pressed hard against the porcelain of the sink while he regarded himself in the mirror for almost an hour. It had not felt so long. He had not had more than five or six drinks; a calm night by all accounts after his days as a student. *I need to get home. Now.* As he emerged back into the reception room the crowd was significantly lighter than it had been when he'd disappeared. His mouth was dry from not having had anything during his freak-out. He b-lined towards the bar area for a drink of water before he left and heard Reuben's loud voice calling his name. At first he made the decision to pretend he hadn't heard it. The call became louder and now apparently included Tom's voice as well. Jon turned his head while he walked and waved a quick wave while signalling his intent to get another drink. He felt the splinters of pain in his neck as he turned his head and twisted his wrists a little when they had returned to his sides.

Without speaking to the bartender or server, Jon grabbed a glass from over the bar and walked to the end where several pitchers of ice-water were ready. He filled his glass and quickly drained the contents. He did the same again. On his third glass he slowed and heard his friends calling again. This time it included the small voice of Reuben's new *girlfriend*. It was too much. His understanding of the world as it had been before Fiona had died was disappearing. Without turning to face his callers, Jon walked quickly around the bar and found the nearest exit into the parking lot. Even the sky looked different as he looked upwards and took a deep breath.

---

13 - September 2nd – Fiona

Geoff had volunteered to drive her to work for her first day back. They talked about Jonathan in the car. Fiona talked about work in the car. They listened to music that Geoff clearly didn't know.

- He came to see me at work a lot, it was really nice.
- Yea? It's usually so hard for people to pry him out of his office once his work day starts.
- Hmm. Yea. This was back when he worked out of the university, though. His office was, like, 200 feet from the Special Collections room.

Geoff smiled with a sense of intermittent calmness as he drove. He was worried though, that he would be driving too quickly or do anything that was too familiar. Fiona sat still in the passenger seat with her feet rooted to the ground in front of her. Her seatbelt was, of course, in the proper position and she stared out of the window while they chatted together. Geoff had driven twenty minutes out of his way to pick her up and take her the ten-minute drive to work. Neither of them were quite sure yet what Fi was going to do about getting to work herself in the future. She could move, or she could drive, but neither seemed like a topic worth bringing up just yet.

- You know that people are going to ask you things today, right?
- I know.

69

She had thought about it. She still stared out of the window and smiled about it a little bit. Turning her head to look at her father in law while he drove she said:

- I miss him every day, more than I can deal with. But pretending he wasn't ever here, or not talking about him... well then he would really be totally gone. Right?
- Okay.
- It's going to be really difficult, yea. But I love him and I want to talk about him.

Geoff smiled and winced slightly as he drove. The steering wheel wobbled a little as he clenched his fist and turned the wrinkled skin of his knuckles white. He exhaled hard and made a noise of groaning relief. When he turned to face Fiona it was clear he was crying a little but he did not lose his smile.

- I'm really proud of you Fiona.

She smiled back as they pulled into the parking lot of the University library. Lots of students were milling around, most with headphones in. The sky was a light shade of grey, but almost everyone wore sunglasses. Fiona gathered her things in the front seat of the car and went to get out and say goodbye with a peck on the cheek to her father-in-law.

- Hang on. I'm taking you all the way in darling.
- What? No. You don't have to do that.
- I know I don't bloody have to. I want to. You never invite me to come and see where you work. This might be my only chance!

He was messing with her and she knew it, but she was happy he would take her all the way to her little room.

He walked in with his hands in his pockets, apparently uncomfortable in the university environment. Geoffrey Eliot had never been to university back in his day; he had married Clara instead and worked his whole life. Fiona dropped her

70

things off at her little desk and offered to show him around. There was nobody in the special collections department yet as they had arrived before it was due to open. Usually Alex would swing by right as the clock ticked past nine in the morning whether it was just to say hi or to stay for the day and make the place her own as usual. She apparently hadn't been in at all during Fiona's absence. They had hired some student-intern to bridge the gap during Fiona's absence and things looked better than she had expected. She felt like a child showing her grandfather how tidy she could keep her room.

- Well. I'm glad you're alright. And I'm glad you let me see where you work.
- Thanks for the ride Geoff. Do you know how to get back out to the parking lot?
- I'll figure it out. I'm a university guy now!

He smiled and hugged her before walking out with his hands once again thrust in his deep jacket pockets.

Fiona went about her morning routine with remarkable ease. It was as though she hadn't left – if she did not count all the things that were slightly in the wrong place thanks to the intern doing her best in Fi's absence. She turned her computer on, looked at the cart containing the various texts that needed re-shelving and sat in her chair with her hands clasped around her travel-mug and her shoulders hunched forwards as though she was trying to steal the warmth escaping her drink. As her screen clicked on, she started her log-in sequence and waited for the prehistoric technology to catch up with her. Reflexively she checked her phone and sent Jonathan a text: "Morning darling, hope work is good. Xx." She was in the midst of checking several emails that needed catching up with before she realized her mistake. The text remained a blue bubble on the screen floating alone without a "delivered" notification beneath it. She stopped in her seat for a few minutes and just looked at the screen until it darkened and eventually went black. There was still nobody in the department. It was a Wednesday morning so most students were probably still hungover from all of the Tuesday night frivolities – it really could have been any morning. Alex was usually her first customer. She needed a reply to a text. It was a fix. Jonathan never failed to reply so this was infuriating and made her feel uneasy. She texted Alex to ask if she was coming by. It was like heroin when her phone finally buzzed and she made contact with her friend. Even though she was not going to be over until later in the afternoon, Fiona felt immeasurably better. She was able to continue with her work as normal, silently wishing that voicemail was still a thing so that she could hear Jonathan's voice quickly at work like widows in Hollywood movies did.

The day passed with relative ease. Her work kept her mind busy. She thought of things she would tell Jonathan when she got home. Every time, she managed to catch herself and issue a quick reminder that she would no longer be able to do that. Surprisingly, she became more exhausted at the constant self-reminders and personal stability checks than actually upset. That being said, it was her first day back at work for quite some time and she was still not sleeping through the night. When they had started dating they had spent nights apart, but both soon became ill-at-ease without the company of the other overnight. Fiona had made her claim for a solid eighty-percent of the real-estate of Jonathan's bed while they slept, ensuring that he stayed flat on his back or front without moving too much once they had drifted off. It seemed to be that his own unease would cease somewhat when they went to sleep. The lines on his face and the whites on his knuckles from whatever stressors plagued him that day would soften and he would breathe more calmly. Whatever plagued him never truly disappeared. *He never seems to sleep as well he should.* Fiona spent the time before drifting off being gently touched by Jonathan in his half-awake state. He would rub her back softly, often for hours, or play with her hair gently until he felt her move slightly with the erratic nature indicative of being caught in a dream. When she was gone, he could let himself go, too.

They had become more adept at spending nights apart after a few years when they had to. Fiona would enjoy spending evenings at Alex and Tom's but would struggle to fall asleep without Jonathan's company. His unease gave her a sense of purpose. He was meant to rub her back. His purpose, then, was hers; was her.

Fiona lost herself in good memories between the bookshelves of the special collections room. She was humming along to the classical music that played quietly in the background so as to soften or mute the harsh sounds of pages turning at each desk. She was warm and briefly felt Jonathan's hand on her back as though she was sleeping. Her work day had moved quickly and Alex had yet to come by; she was looking forward to seeing her friend.

- Hey babe.

Fi recognized the voice immediately. Alex had issued the greeting out into the ether of the small room without even knowing if Fiona was in there. There were no other students in there for Alex to disrupt, but it was certainly not as though she had checked. As per the usual, she began unpacking her several bags of books and notes along with a laptop that looked close to death after having been squashed between lunches, coffee mugs, and crumpled textbooks in her backpack.

- Hey I wasn't sure if you were going to swing by after all.

Fi emerged from between the shelves carrying some smaller documents. She had yet to figure out where they were meant to go and her mind just was not up for the troubleshooting that the problem called for; she placed them on her desk to be confused about later.

- I need to get the number or the email address of the kid who worked here while I was gone...I kind of expected him or her to be here for a little while as like an overlap when I got back so that they could explain anything that had gone wrong or needs changing.
- Oh did they fuck everything up?

Fiona laughed at her friend's bluntness and looked around.

- No. Not exactly fucked up. It's just annoying because they obviously do some of the little things a bit differently to how I've been doing them for years.
- Oh yea.
- Yea it's tripping me up.
- Well that's shit.
- Sure. It's a bit shit.

Alex busied herself with setting up her things to do a little bit of work. It was, however, almost 4:30 and Fi knew that it was uncharacteristic of Alex to "post-up" anywhere unless she could reasonably put in a few hours of work. With the special collections department closing in an hour or so, and neither of them having any intention of staying late, Fiona knew that she was there for company. She said nothing. She silently appreciated the gesture and returned to shelving. After finding homes for a few journals she heard the familiar drone of Alex's headphones escaping the sockets of her ears and rendering the classical background music useless. *How is this girl not deaf yet?*

At a few minutes before the end of the working day for Fiona's little slice of the library, all work had ceased between her and Alex and they occupied the time by talking about Alex's thesis. This was safe. Technically, according to Alex this counted as work for her so she didn't have to feel bad about wasting any time that could have been better used studying, and it also kept the various demons at bay that she was sure were working their way through Fiona's mind about going home to an empty house for the first time after work.

- I'd ask you if you want to get a drink after work today but I've got to meet Tom for some work thing or other.
- No that's fine. I'm pretty tired anyway. Not working for weeks on end takes its toll once you get back to it apparently.
- Yea, lazy bitch, you'll get back into it soon enough.

They both laughed a little before their conversation was interrupted by a student who must have only been the third or fourth visitor of the day.

- Hi can you help me out really quickly.

Alex took the lead with a nonchalance that Fiona neglected to challenge.

- What do you need? It's like one minute until the department closes eh.
- Oh. Okay. That's fine I'll come back tomorrow.

The girls laughed acknowledging Alex's bluntness and quickly apologized and offered to help again.

- No. No.

He paused again and looked firmly at the ground some ten feet ahead of him.

- No. I'll come back another time. Not important.

It seemed best to just let him go. Many of the grad students who needed the materials from the special collections department spent so much time cooped up in small offices or in their bedrooms working on problems or ideas for such long periods of time that they did not deal well with human interaction when it was required of them. This poor guy was no different.

His windbreaker shuffled audibly as he stood in the doorway before uncomfortably gesturing that he was going to leave. Both women watched him walk by the glass wall of the department until he was out of view. His gaze remained fixed on the ground and he shuffled with the urgency of a child desperate to use the toilet but too embarrassed to ask to do so.

- I feel bad for not helping the guy. Probably took him all he had to come in here and ask for help.
- Whatever, he said he'd be back tomorrow. You can enjoy that one all by yourself!

Alex laughed without looking up while packing her bags and preparing to leave.

- How are you getting home tonight babe?
- Geoff is taking me again.

Alex looked up making a face suggestive of an "aww" sound before hugging Fiona and getting on her way. As the rest of the library remained open until much later, there were still plenty of students milling around outside the door of the special collections department. Fiona watched her friend bustle through the crowd, catching the corners of her many bags of books on unsuspecting undergrads as she waded confidently towards wherever she needed to go.

Geoffrey had opted not to come in to pick Fiona up at the end of the day. He had made the excuse that he didn't want to embarrass her in front of her friends. She suspected that although he may have believed this to be partly true, he had probably forgotten how to get to her department or felt intimidated by the thousands of students. Fi waved to him while walking towards the car at the end of the day. The sky stayed red throughout the drive home while she stared from the window.

---

14 - September 30ᵗʰ – Jonathan

His hair was getting long. He had maintained his beard a little for the reception the previous week, but his homeless-vibe was really starting to show through. Jon had decided to rent a car so that he would be able to get around by himself, a move that most chose to see as a step in the right direction. He saw it as a means to avoid the inevitable questioning that friends or family would berate him with on car journeys should he need a ride anywhere. He knew they meant well, but he still hated it.

- Well that's new.

His dad regarded the car as Jon pulled into his parents' driveway. Jon sat behind the wheel of an older dark green BMW 3-Series with a grey leather interior.

- I thought you'd have been finished with the three series trend after the last one mate.

Jon shrugged off the comment and hugged his dad. Geoff's smile waned slightly as he acknowledged his son's blank expression. He was not wrong. The car was basically identical to his old one that killed his wife and did its best to take Jon, too. Geoff decided it wasn't worth dwelling on right away.

- Your mum's glad you've come by. She says you've been working way too much.
- Yea it's been busy, it's not her by any means. She knows that.
- Hmm.

77

Jon followed his dad through to the kitchen where he had introduced Fiona to his parents almost three years ago. Clara was talking loudly on the phone to a friend that Jon was probably supposed to have known but quickly cut the conversation short when the two men joined her in the kitchen. Her face beamed and she drew Jon in for a hug. She busied herself with asking him a thousand mundane questions while putting the kettle on and not waiting for answers. Jon quickly got the recap of all the family friends he had not heard from or spoken to in a while and nodded along with the one-sided conversation. His father remained on the periphery of the conversation idly checking his phone with a trumpet-effect as he did his best to focus his eyes on the small text.

- So Jill's oldest had her baby this week. Two weeks early believe it or not. I think that'll be it for work for her now. I don't think she ever planned on going back after she had it...

It was easy for Jon to follow the conversation and his mum was clearly enjoying the 'catching up' they were doing. While uninterested in Jill's daughter's baby — so much so that he had forgotten quickly if it was a boy or a girl — he appreciated the sentiment behind the white noise that his mum knew she was offering.

Jon regarded his dad briefly during the "monologue." Geoffrey looked tired. Like Jonathan, he looked much bigger than he actually was. His shoulders bore the appearance of strength, with a rounded posture to complement his age. What had once been strong was now replaced with the wisdom of experience. His eyes failed him somewhat while he stared at the screen of his phone. He drew it back and forth to bring the screen into focus while he absent-mindedly listened to his wife catching up with his oldest son. Forty years of marriage was something to be proud of. Geoff was evidently a grateful man. Although he had earned everything he had, it seemed as though he thought he was always pretending. Jon watched closely and recognized the additional weight that his own life had forced on his father of late. This was a time when Geoffrey and Clara were meant to relax, talk about other people's kids and grandkids, patiently wait for a cancer diagnosis, and enjoy dwindling work schedules before eventually making the G&T that would take them into full retirement. He evidently had none of that on his mind. His mind was burdened by the course his son's life had taken. He couldn't understand why it had gone such a way.

Jon had been proud of his father's relationship with Fiona. After being so nervous for his family to make introductions with her, things had seemed to go so well. *Maybe dad wanted a daughter.* Kathy had been all Fiona had since she was a young teenager, so by the time she had met Geoff there must have been a dad-shaped hole in her life at least somewhere. Geoff's hair had been gone for some years by this point. He had joked that this was on purpose; that real men suck the hair back in as anyone can simply *grow it themselves.* The lines around his eyes distinctly matched the map of the same lines recently deepening on Jonathan's own face. Unlike Jon's, his father's eyes remained blue while Jon's frequently appeared grey under most light.

- Where's David today anyway?
- Apparently off on some trip for university. I would have thought it would just be regular classes by this time of year though. I don't ask anymore.

At twenty-one, David was in his last year of a business degree. Jon had seen him just once or twice in the last year despite the fact that he lived at his parents' house. They were not estranged or distant, rather, they simply had very little to talk about. He had stood in the same circle after Fiona was buried and they all wore black several months earlier.

Clara's monologue had slowed to a trot and they talked more candidly. She began to show that she had been upset that Jon hadn't visited as often as she would have liked. Jon knew, however, that this was made only marginally worse by the fact that Fiona was no longer with him. *It's weird that she's not here right now. I haven't dealt with Mum directly for ages.* Clara would have been upset that Jon was not visiting regardless as he rarely did. His work kept him busy despite his best intentions. It always seemed as though whatever time spent with his family had been overflow from the effort he spent on Fiona; a characteristic that neither she, nor his parents appreciated or fully understood. *She'd be at work right now. I should be at work right now.* His cup of tea was cold and only half-gone. In a partially self-harming sort of manner, he downed the rest of the cup quickly so as to not have to squeeze past his mum by the sink to pour it out. This would have inevitably caused an onslaught of "why didn't you finish that" or "are you eating enough" questions that he was in no mood to answer. It was always tea with his mum and dad. They'd been Fiona's converters in the matter. Before Scotland, Fiona's preferences lay with coffee or some weird bag of potpourri dunked in hot water that she called tea. Geoff and Clara had set her right on the latter and she had developed a taste for cheap, supermarket-brand teabags.

She was standing at the door in the kitchen, then. Her hands were clasped gently around a cup of tea while she stared at Jonathan listening to his mum talk. She mouthed something silently across the room and Jon mimed a small kiss back to her. Her hair was long; they were not yet married. They had not yet even thought about it. No vacancy at all was present in her eyes as she looked down towards the table at which Jonathan sat quietly. She wanted to sit on his lap but was unsure about how his parents would see such a move. It was her spot. Jonathan wanted her to but knew she would never actually do it. They would make up for it after leaving.

Jon was quickly compelled to leave. His dad quickly sensed his irritability and broached the subject first to shift blame away from his son and prevent Clara from asking why.

- You off mate?
- In a bit yea. Gotta' get back to work. Got a few emails since I've been here that need answering.

Yea I have to go. She'll be waiting.

- Alright darling.

Surprisingly, his mother offered no restraints, guilt trips, or coercions aimed at making him stay, nor did she try to give him food or offer him to have a meal with them. She knew. That was good. Having not removed his jacket since sitting down, Jon stood up slowly and made for the front door with both his parents in tow. While he put his boots on and they watched his moves, he broke the silence so as to not simply be observed.

- See Roob's gone all domestic now eh.
- Oh, Karen?
- You knew about her?
- He's been with her for a few months now I guess. They started seeing each other right after Fiona died I think.

Clara's blunt expression, however well meaning, caused an almost noticeable wince in each of the men's faces. Jon was usually comfortable when talking about death. *People won't even say stuff like "oh, he died." Now it's like "Oh, he's passed on;" or not even that: "he's passed…" Well what the fuck has he "passed?" Did he pass gas?*

It had seemed ridiculous before. But, like everything, it changes when it becomes personal.

- Yea, well it was news to me. Seems like he's doing well, though.

Well. Fuck. Jon's heart sped up a little and he got a little warm standing in the doorway to his parents' house. He hugged them both and made for his car, conscious of the beads of sweat beginning to appear on his forehead. The scars on his back radiated beneath his shirt as he started the engine and backed out of the driveway. His déjà vu would have been uncanny had the passenger seat beside him been filled. It should not have bothered him that Reuben had a girlfriend; that he knew. He hadn't actually received any emails from work and his parents probably knew that, but saying "hey, I'm fucking tired of being here, I'm uncomfortable, stressed, and I don't give a shit about the people you are telling me about" seemed a little rude. He did love his parents, but listening to the lives of others was merely an unwelcome reminder that life went on.

---

15 - September 30th – Fiona

Life was certainly going on. There really was no stopping it. Work had settled into a routine that functioned well. Having left the apartment she once shared with her husband, Fiona had moved closer to the university so that she would have to neither drive nor rely on public transport. She doubted that she would ever drive again and saw no immediate need to do so. Even riding as a passenger was usually too much depending on with whom she drove. Her walk to work in the morning and home took less than twenty minutes and, when the sun shone, she could look up at the sky and get some use out of the sunglasses she had assumed would remain in their case during her time in Scotland. It rained often but she seemed not to notice. Jonathan's apartment – she no longer called it home – had been taken over quickly and she had just as quickly found her new place. It was small and cramped. No space for yoga but in the small strip of carpeted space between the foot of her bed and her cupboard, but it worked. The sheets she had shared with Jonathan were worn well by the same bed in a new room. Despite several months having passed, she was sure they still kept his smell.

Her collection of clothes overflowed the tiny dresser-cupboard crossover that came with the semi-furnished apartment. She could no longer reap the benefits of the eighty-twenty split of the space in Jonathan's closet and was instead forced to make-do in the one bedroom apartment sized storage space. Alex had already joked that a new man was certainly needed to remedy such a problem, and to her surprise, Fiona had not become upset or offended at the remark. She was by no means ready for such a step, but the comical sentiment meant a lot at the time. Since living alone, she adapted to the way that life worked and felt bad about the various benefits that such a living situation afforded. Of course, she felt the pangs of sadness and irritation at the things that now took twice as long. Crying daily was still something she dealt with. She had been caught crying at work more than once since she had returned, and more than once she had been caught crying when she didn't even realize that she was.

- Excuse me.
- Yes, what can I help you with.
- Are you Okay?
- Yes, why?

It had become a conversation that she now anticipated. The strange looks she once received for her apparent vacancy had been replaced with looks of concern or compassion by passersby hoping to help or understand what she must have been going through. Fiona also realised that she could be prone to accidentally crying even if she was smiling; something she had previously thought impossible, yet still the pages of various journals and texts at work became accidentally wetted.

The background picture on her phone screen broke a rule she had maintained since phones could even take pictures, as she had a selfie shot of Jonathan and her walking downtown in Edinburgh on a particularly cold day. Her hair had been long; they must have either just gotten married or not been married by that point. Jonathan's face bore a smile that, for most, would be considered limited or restricted in some way. Fiona knew this was about as widespread as his face would go. It was the best kind of smile he could afford when feeling content in such a way. When she locked her phone, a picture of herself, Geoff, Clara, David, Jonathan, and her mum together stared back at her. Kathy had been planning to come over to see her daughter again before Jonathan died. When he did, her plans changed and she nearly jumped on a flight right away to comfort her daughter. Now, however, she was planning to bring Fiona *home* to Portland. *Portland wasn't home, though.* Portland had not been home for Fi in years. Even when she had grown up there in a suburb things had not felt like home. She had doubted upon moving to Scotland that anywhere really would, and even as she walked to work from her new apartment to her comfortable little job at the university she was not sure that Scotland actually did yet either.

I really can't afford to head back to Portland at the moment.

- Geoffrey needs me here, mum. I just took ages off of work after Jonathan. If I leave again they're going to get really pissed off. And rightly so.
- Please don't use words like that. But Okay.

Kathy had been known to apologize profusely for using a word with the scathing seriousness of "crap" or "damn" in the past. It was easy to filter one's language for use around children or teenagers, but Fiona had warned Jonathan prior to meeting her mum that this kind of filter would need to be on overdrive. He undoubtedly slipped up repeatedly.

- What if you came home for Christmas? I never get to see you and you'll probably get some time off from work anyway, right?
- You know I miss you. I'll do my best and see what it's like for time off and flights and everything. Okay?

This was enough to pacify Kathy for a while, but Fi also knew that this would just send her into planning overload-mode and she would soon have a detailed itinerary of a trip that may never even happen anyway. *If it makes her happy at the moment, it's fine.*

Work was going slowly. There were a few of the regular students from the Theology and Divinity department taking up several of the desk cubicles in the corner working quietly. She was still able to text Alex and Tom throughout the day to pass the time. It was early in the semester so most of the students were fairly respectful in terms of replacing materials and putting things back where they found them if they only used them for a short amount of time. As things became more overwhelming in the students' schedules, so too did the mess in the special collections department from people just discarding texts in a rush between study sessions. Fiona found herself almost looking forward to such a time as there would, at least, be things for her to do throughout the day. Alex couldn't come by this time as she was just too busy preparing for an interview session she was planning for a few weeks later. Confident in the knowledge that there really was nothing to do, Fiona took her little notebook and fountain pen from her purse. It had been a gift from Jonathan a long time ago, but she had rarely used its pages for the fear that whatever she had chosen to write may have tainted the gift had it been inadequate.

- Hello.

She hardly heard it the first time.

- Excuse me.

It was louder now, but still with the definite concern that a call too loud in a library setting would be in some way offensive. Fiona got up from her desk and peered around the shelves at the doorway of the special collections department. Walking briskly away, but still visible through the one glass wall of the room, was the source of the voice. She recognized him quickly and trotted over to the door to call him back. After he didn't answer her call he seemed to speed up but Fiona felt compelled to catch him and offer her help.

She was just a foot or so away from him still calling out to him before he turned around and acknowledged her again. She did not know his name so she could just apologize.

- What do you need today?

She spoke with a smile on her face that permeated her tone.

- I remember you from a few weeks ago. I'm sorry I missed you today I just couldn't hear you. You know that you can come into special collections without asking though, right?

He looked about twenty-four; maybe a little bit older. His windbreaker shuffled as he walked but he made no real response to Fiona's efforts to catch up with him and help. She did not notice his lack of words, it was not uncommon for students like this to visit her department and be terrified of a member of the opposite sex standing in their way of the materials they needed. She was also concerned that he still needed the same item that he had been looking for some weeks ago. *I hope this poor kid hasn't failed some assignment because he was too embarrassed to ask for what he needed because of me... or because of Alex last time. Better not let this guy catch me crying. It would probably break the poor bastard.*

Ever so quietly, the student explained what he needed to Fiona while repeatedly looking over at the group of students in the corner. They paid him no attention, but he seemed concerned that they would hear what he had asked for as if this was something terrible. The texts he needed were, for the special collections department, not that obscure or uncommon. There were even several copies of one of the journals that he wanted to use.

- I'm really sorry that it's taken so long to help you out with these. I hope it didn't affect any assignments you had due.
- It's fine.

He evidently was not a man of many words. Fiona stood a few inches shorter than the guy but he seemed so much smaller than her thanks to his posture and his countenance. She tried to stop her face from expressing the feelings of pity she felt towards this guy. It was still weird that he didn't have a bag or any thing that he could work with at all. This was explained quickly when he walked away after saying "bye" just about as quietly as one could utter the word. He obviously did not realize that materials from this department had to stay there. Unlike the rest of the library, students could not withdraw books or journals or texts. All studying had to be done in the department itself. If small amounts of text were needed, Fiona would always photocopy particular pages provided it would not damage the material during the copy process. Some of the oldest texts in her department were only available under supervised appointment.

- Hey. Um. Sorry.

She followed him again quickly before he got out of the door. He seemed to walk in a rush all the time. His face even expressed a sense of unexplained urgency that made her pity him more and feel even worse when she told him that the materials could not leave.

- You'll have to study that stuff here actually. I can make copies of things if you need me to, though.

He shuffled on the spot a little and passed his left hand anxiously over his other arm where Fiona had gently grabbed him to get his attention and stop him from leaving. Without saying anything and instead nodding slightly in apology, he walked back to the long desk in the centre of the department and opened one of his newly acquired books to an apparenrty random page and started reading immediately.

- Okay.

Fiona paused and watched him for a few seconds.

- You will let me know if you need anything won't you? I can get you some paper and a pen if you need to take notes. Or you can check out a laptop from upstairs and bring it down here to work if you need to.
- I'm fine.

She was glad she had helped, but it seemed as though the poor guy still felt awfully uncomfortable sat alone in the middle of the room apparently reading important material.

By the end of the day the 5:20 announcement that the department would be closing in ten minutes had crept up on everyone working in the special collections room. The group of theology students mumbled amongst themselves and quietly packed their things. Fiona watched as the young man in his windbreaker – which he had not removed in the hours he had been sat reading – heard the announcement and promptly closed his book, placed it atop the pile on the desk he was using, and walked out without saying a word. His shuffle was somewhat more relaxed upon leaving; almost as though he had reached a realization about something that he had needed for a while in his work. She wondered quietly if he was one of the brilliant students able to see something once and recall it forever like some sort of eidetic or photographic memory. He was certainly weird enough to fit the bill – harmless all the same.

True to form, Fiona watched the door at 5:30 for the occasional trickle of desperate students needing help at the last minute, but also for the chance that Jonathan would meet her from work. Like his dad, his hands would be in his pockets while he waited, but he would by no means feel out of place. He was taller than most of the students and occasionally seemed to tower over Fiona. With his beard and the lines in his face by the end of the day he often looked a great deal older than he was.

- Hey darling.

She would turn slowly, knowing his deep voice and instantly sensing his smell in the room.

- Hey. Let me clean up real' quick and we can get going.
- Don't rush babe. I like seeing you do your thing at work.

It was true. He had mentioned it lots of times that he enjoyed seeing her work in the library.

- Are you going to be reading these books and stuff for your own degree soon, though?

Jonathan was hardly wealthy based on his salary from the university and the small cheques he picked up for freelance work, but he had wanted Fiona to go back to school ever since she had mentioned completing her PhD after just a few months of their being together.

Jonathan did not come this time, but thankfully neither did any last minute requests from students. She walked to the door to lock it to the outside while she organized her things and left some notes for herself for the following morning. At the door she looked to see the weather outside through the window down the hall. It was raining; hard. The sun still shone thanks to the long summer days, but even this would be coming to an end soon. She would have to ready herself again for the cold winter that Scotland offered. *Portland is worse in the winter I'm sure.* Her walk was not marred by the rain, instead the grey of the sky that overpowered the sun seemed to stretch on further than she had noticed before. It seemed to wrap around the horizon in the distance that she could observe between the buildings on the way home as if to offer a sense of infinite and curvature she could not understand. Fiona walked briskly through the rain and the grey to the home in which she had squeezed her little existence for the time being. The pictures of Jonathan on the wall were enough to make her smile and cry when she walked in. The house smelled of his clothes while she made some coffee and sat down to read. She missed him with every part of her. *I need to have some friends over here soon. We can all laugh about the size of my little apartment.*

---

16 - October 25th – Jonathan

- Mate, pick up your fucking phone. I'm tired of this horseshit. Your dad's been ringing me non-fucking-stop for like the last week asking what's going on. Don't be a cock.

Roob's message once again went unanswered. Tom had tried the same. Geoff had done the rounds and ensured that Jon was not passed out in his house somewhere and checked with work to see if anyone had seen him recently. They knew he was alright; not dead or disappeared at least. For the last few weeks the flowers on Fiona's grave had been renewed almost daily. Geoff knew this would not have been Roob, and had checked with Alex to see when she had been now that she was out and about and talking to people a little more freely. Tom had been dealing with everything else a lot better since Alex had come out of relative hiding. She seemed as though she was going to be okay, at least with time.

Jon's phone was rarely switched on at this point. He made contact with work via email; even that was rare. He had been so busy with the assignments and projects on which he had been working for months that he felt contact was not at all necessary.

- He's working hard at least. It could be worse. He could be just moping at home.
- Yea you're right. I'll lay off him for a wee bit then.

Conversations between Jon's friends and family now rarely included him but always involved him. He made enough contact with everyone to prove he was alright, but would quickly get angry when asked why he was not coming out or why nobody got to see him anymore. People were evidently getting closer and closer to the point at which they would finally break and explain that had been *long enough*. It had not. It had by no means been long enough for anything. What was long enough? He really couldn't have done it right either way.

Jon sat quietly at his desk as usual at around eleven in the morning. Crushing a handful of painkillers sloppily under a full mug of coffee, he watched as several drips made their way down the side of his mug while others landed in brown, circular stains on what was probably important work. He exhaled and regarded his mass of crumpled work before sweeping the crushed and powdery white mess into his mug and downing its contents – it was cold, but he had not noticed. The mug itself had the bottom third of its handle missing from a previous drop or accident in recent weeks and had not been washed since its last use. He would have tasted everything had he been present for his drink. Jon leaned back and stared at the mountain of books and papers strewn across his little desk. Perhaps this was the better side of the deal he received with Fiona as she had confidently commandeered the majority share of the closet real-estate. A small pile of her work, probably from university days, rested unharmed on the corner of the desk. A small canyon of dark, wooden, empty space separated her work from his so there was no chance he would ruin anything. *She may still need it. She'll be pissed if I mess it up. She wouldn't say anything if she was, though.* His laptop keyboard could no longer be seen beneath the various papers; it was there, though. He looked at everything with a cursory glance and wondered why, in a time when just about everything could be done on his computer and then emailed, he still had such an abundance of paper. Some of the documents were mottled with red marks; the evidence of student work that could have been done better. Other pages bore the stains of coffee from more than just his most recent cup. He had books opened to pages he was sure he had not read before, but they must have been important or they wouldn't have been left in such a way. A small pile of essays on the far side of his desk moved slightly from the vibration of his phone beneath it. For a few seconds he thought about answering it. It made him anxious; he felt rooted to his chair, stuck between the desire to lean forward and make actual contact with someone else and the overwhelming pressure to stay in this state and listen to the sounds of Fiona walking around the house. His heartbeat raced and he faintly heard the sounds of hospital machines from far away. The weird feelings of cognitive dissonance from wanting to do two opposing things or holding two opposing beliefs had become commonplace for him.

Finally, the pages stopped moving. Jon leant forwards slowly and carelessly brushed the concealing papers aside. He took his phone in his hand and pressed the button to reveal who had bothered him. There were a few too many notifications to bother looking through so he quickly unlocked and then locked his phone revealing the background picture of Fiona laying on the beach in Spain. Based on the light and the direction from which the picture was taken, only he knew that she was topless in the picture. It was a combination of tastefully done and childishly kept. He felt his dick twitch and swell a little as he thought more about it, then immediately felt sick. He was sure this was just a result of the combination of painkillers he had just taken finally working their way past the actual points of discomfort in his back and wrists and eventually numbing his face to the point that it no longer felt like his own. He screamed loudly but could only just hear the sound as he violently swept everything from his desk. The scream brought the blood to the front of his face as it had when he was a child being told to put on sunscreen or get in the car to go somewhere he hated. The whites of his cheeks became flushed as he screamed yet his ears rendered it almost noiseless even in the silence of his office. His head throbbed dully.

Jon's desk was just about empty. When his complexion had settled and his ears began to return to life, he saw his mess. Calmly, he collected the pile of books and papers Fiona had been saving placed them carefully back on the corner of the desk where she had left them. No spots of coffee had been bold enough to tarnish them in the hurricane he had caused. The rest of his work and his probably broken computer lay on the floor next to the capsized coffee mug slowly and silently dripping the remaining brown ooze of whatever had been crushed into it. Jon walked calmly down the hall to take a shower, removing his shirt on the way and carefully hanging it on the back of a chair in the dining area. He had way too much to do to care about a little mess in his office.

- Roob? What are you up to mate?
- Jon?
- No. Yea who the fuck did you think it was. Why do people still ask that when it says who's calling on their damn screen.
- Well you sound like you're in a good mood again.
- Look do you want to go for a drink or not?
- Like now? It's 11:30 in the morning. And its Tuesday.

The conversation was getting annoying for Jon. He had expected a warm welcome back into the outside world if he finally made contact. He had evidently pissed Reuben off more than he had initially thought. *He'll get over it.*

- No, not like *right now*. Let's get drinks later in the week. It'd be good to see some people.

Reuben was evidently wary. Jon sensed his apprehension through the phone, and also heard movement in the background.

- Karen there right now?
- Why?
- Aren't you at work?

Jon quickly felt anxious and regretted calling. He had not forgotten about Reuben and Karen, and it shouldn't have even bothered him, but he had also not anticipated her being present on the other end of the phone when he rang. Reuben was evidently not at work. *Must be nice for some people not to have to work.* Roob was able to calm down the situation he felt was boiling up to something out of nothing, though.

- Yea. Sounds like a good night mate. Let's do something Friday. I'll give Tom a ring. Alex would come out if he did, too.
- Yea. Alright wicked mate.

Several hours later Roob had done the usual and called several people they knew to go out on the weekend for some much needed drinks. He obviously anticipated some sort of apology from Jon about his messed-up, reclusive behavior. No such apology would come from Jon but the sentiment of wanting to see people would have to be enough.

Jon stood in front of the mirror some three days later on the afternoon before he would be going out. Perhaps this would be a second audition after his failed attempt at Toni and Dave's reception. His beard needed to be tamed and he was in desperate need of a haircut. He knew that, had he been working somewhere that actually required his presence, he would not have been able to let himself go quite so badly. The bathroom counter was mottled with the various makeup and bathroom products Fiona had left half-finished. Everything was left as it was. Jon had cleaned, of course, but was careful to put things back exactly in the spots in which they had been left. After a quick songless shower, Jon clicked his electric

95

beard trimmer on to start taking care of the wayward nature of his facial hair. He trimmed it short enough to shave, and then took out his safety razor and did the rest. After being hidden by the beard, his face beneath was pale and almost ghostly. In the grey-blue hue of the bathroom, his skin resembled the skin of a prison inmate's that he had seen on the news; the man in question had evidently evaded or neglected sunlight for years. He noticed how much thinner he had got in just a few months of not caring. *Well everyone's going to think I'm fucking nuts if they see me as I am now.* Fiona had once laughed and made a comment about his face upon seeing it clean shaven; something about how his hair loss didn't match the youth of his face without a beard. Since then he had always kept a short beard.

Pushed to the end of the bathroom counter was a bunched up towel and a pair of socks that Fiona had left. The outline of dust around them was visible as Jon had been afraid to move them during the last few times he had cleaned the bathroom and wiped the counter. Fi had a habit of sitting atop the counter with her feet in the sink full of warm water while she read. Her little feet would be a dark shade of red on her walk back to their bedroom and he would steal their heat on his own feet as she climbed into bed with him. Jon left the bathroom and returned with a clean hand towel with which to wipe his face after shaving. His skin reddened against the coarse fabric of the towel, bringing it to life a little. He felt slightly better, which would be useful for the expression on his face when he would later have to convince his friends that he actually was feeling better. *There was nothing worse than pity. He could almost feel the condescension already.* He passed his hands over his now clean shaven face and regarded the small fleck scars once again up his forearms. He knew they were there, but doubted if anyone else would notice them if they did not know about his year. *I look fourteen. I need a haircut.*

Karen was pleasant. Jon was polite. Tom and Alex were quiet but enjoyed being out. They talked of Fiona a lot and of how she would have enjoyed being there. Jon neither winced nor fell out of place into his recently common state of absence. They drank together at the new brew pub which, as was predicted by Jon, no longer smelled of the MDF-wood and plaster of its renovation. Karen seemed to go well with Roob, and he hadn't changed as a result of his new relationship, at least not in any noticeable or negative way. Karen waved hello to several friends passing by their table throughout the night, she apparently knew many more people there than the rest of them. Some girl named Tess stopped by at several points and Jon had nodded politely upon introductions. She eventually meandered off to her own group of friends and Karen bid her a polite adieu. Jon Eliot sat back and watched the scene through glassy eyes. There were enough people at their table to allow him to speak less frequently and pass the social experiment with nods and smiles much more appropriately. He instead lived comfortably in the space behind his eyes and the space inside his glass.

- See there's been more attacks over there again. I didn't hear how many people this time.
- Yea it's crazy eh. I heard that on the radio, too.

The conversation was the same. The world was going on and nobody was upset with Jon for letting it. He had plenty going on, too much to do, and no intention of jumping into a political discussion about which he had very little interest. In the past he would have watched as Fiona had passionately defended her position, usually against Roob, and then watched her listen to Alex clarify everything with a simplicity that silenced the table and impressed everyone. They had worked well together. Such a conversation would have led to a taxi discussion between Jon and Fi about her going back to school. They both knew it was what she wanted.

The beers in Jon's grasp replaced themselves with an automatism that was somewhat eerie. It had passed habitual much earlier in the evening. He felt relaxed behind the glass of his eyes. The volume of the group had become louder as they continued to drink. Several of Karen's friends had come and gone in the time they had been there. Tom looked drunk. Alex followed suit. Roob remained loud. Karen sipped what may have been the same glass of wine she had bought some hours ago. The condensation on the glass had vanished entirely and the pale Pinot Gris inside it looked tepid and unappetizing; still, she smiled.

- Jon, how's work been going for you mate?

The glass quickly snapped away from his eyes like a door on a starship opening quickly to reveal an enemy behind it. He wondered if he'd paused too long before answering or if it had been smooth.

- Yea, good man. Just the usual.

He realized, as did the rest of the group, how much he was slurring his words. He checked his watch quickly to see that it was still before midnight, before eleven in fact. It was unseemly to be outslurring Reuben by any means, regardless of the time. It did, however, prevent any further questioning about his work. His friends quickly understood that they would likely not receive any clear or coherent answers about his work, and they all knew that they had been asking out of courtesy as it had been some time since they had heard Jon say too much. The starship door closed again, this time as if in slow motion, rendering the noise of the conversation dull and allowing Jon to sit further into the leather-backed stool on which he rested.

- Keep an eye on him later eh, Roob?

- Yea no worries, I got him.

Jon was unaffected by his friends talking about him not five feet away. He sipped his beer and realized that drops were no longer making their way into his mouth. It was evidently time for another. Without a word, he walked over to the bar and bought himself a dark beer. His friends watched as he withdrew his little pill bottle and used his glass to crush several small tablets onto the bar and sweep them into his drink. If they had a problem with his behaviour, they didn't voice it this time. Either that, or he simply couldn't hear it. He felt his back creak, and almost heard it, as he walked back to the table and looked forward to Fiona's warmth in bed when he would arrive home.

---

17 - October 15th – Fiona

It had been a particularly difficult morning routine. Fi had struggled to get out of bed, been off-kilt for the collection of duties she meandered through before leaving for work, and was eventually five or ten minutes late leaving. She knew this would change nothing, but felt uncomfortable nonetheless. Without making coffee at home or stopping for one on the walk to the library, she arrived a few minutes earlier than she normally would have. The smell had been fading from her apartment; the smell she believed still belonged to Jonathan. The pictures on her phone made her sad and happy at the same time. She missed touching his hair in the morning while he pretended to stay asleep next to her until she woke up. She would trace sleep creases that had emerged on his back throughout the night as he rolled onto his side in the morning. Her fingers ran smoothly over his skin and she followed the musculature of his body carefully. It was the best reason to delay getting up and out of bed.

Upon arriving to the special collections department she was surprised to find the door unlocked and the light on. It made her feel uneasy. *Did I leave it unlocked last night? Did someone break in? No, that would be supremely pointless and why would they leave the lights on?* When she got to the door past the glass wall and peered inside, a woman was sitting at her desk working on what looked like a checklist of some kind.

- Um, can I help you?

The girl spun around, obviously shocked at the noise. Fiona had a habit of moving relatively noiselessly thanks to her small stature. Jonathan always said she *padded* rather than walked.

- Hi! Fiona, right?
- Yes?
- I'm Tess. I worked here for a little while when you were on leave.

The young girl offered a hand for Fiona to shake. She promptly took it and the two could relax.

- I just need to get you to sign off on the work that I did while I was here so that I can count it towards my co-op program in library studies. Would that be ok? I hope I didn't leave it too badly in disarray for you.

Fiona laughed.

- No. It was totally fine. Did you enjoy it while you worked here?
- I did, yea. It's a nice place to work. Get's quite quiet but I like that I guess.

Fi signed Tess's form and the two chatted a while about her program and about the work in the SC department.

As Tess was just getting ready to leave, she handed back the keys she was meant to give back weeks ago, and Fiona held them in her hand briefly before thinking out loud quickly. She passed back the keys.

- Hang on, Tess. I might be going away for Christmas to see my mum for a few weeks. *Might be.* This place will be closed for some of it if I do go, but for the rest they will probably need some cover.
- Yea?
- This is rude I guess, but, did they pay you when you covered for me last time?
- They did, but it was a student-slash-co-op rate or something. It basically worked out as a percentage cut on my tuition.

The two women talked for a while about the job and Fiona promised to ask her supervisor about potential casual work for Tess in the library. It would be a great start for her if this was what she planned to do anyway. There were always more qualified people applying for jobs like that but it always turned out that the person who knew someone internally ended up getting the job regardless. It felt nice to be able to actually help someone out in that way. Tess seemed nice enough and had obviously not screwed things up that badly in Fi's absence.

Despite the relative repetitiveness of Fiona's job, in many ways it offered a sense of intrigue on a daily basis. She spent her time nosing through what students had spent their days working on. She had, as a result, learned more by proxy than she really did during her undergrad degree. It had worked out well, although it always left her feeling like she had merely scratched the surface of each of the topics she found herself admiring. It was both extremely exciting for her to be a part of so many fields in this intangible way, but also daunting to know how shockingly little she really understood about so many things. It intimidated her when she thought about going back to school. There were days when it had seemed so appealing. Jonathan's encouragement on the topic could really only go so far, and the conversation had, over the years, slipped into a sense of repetitive comfortability which rendered the plan further away than ever. She wished her legs were resting across his on the couch while they talked. It was a conversation they enjoyed as much as others talked about winning the lottery or selling up and buying a boat somewhere. There was an element of fantasy to it with just enough of a hint of reality to make her heart beat a little faster while he gently stroked her legs.

- Hello?

She recognized the voice and the shuffle of the windbreaker.

True to form, he had no bag or materials for studying. He gestured shyly towards the texts he needed again and collected them himself. For the rest of the day he remained parked in his seat, getting up once after a few hours to either use the bathroom or get some food. Tess had come back around to bring Fiona a cup of coffee and he had not even looked up when she entered. He seemed irritable yet oblivious to most of what was going on around him. Tess made a facial expression upon seeing him that, had Fiona known her better, would have suggested she was as uncomfortable as he was.

- He came in a few times when you were gone. Never has any stuff on him, though.

She whispered so as to not call attention to the young man studying on the other side of the room.

- Oh yeah? He's come by a few times recently, finally got him sorted out with what he needs. I felt bad I couldn't help him out the first time.
- Hmm… He seems creepy. Like, he can't possibly remember everything he's reading but he stays for hours.

- I think he's just super smart.

Fiona laughed. The little guy was certainly creepy, but also harmless. She had talked with him once more in the past few weeks and gotten several more words out of him, but still knew very little. Idle small talk seemed to be a comfortable wheelhouse for both of them while she was working; very little effort was required on her part.

- Anyway, I've got to head off. Thanks again for everything.
- Yea no problem. I'll give you a call or text you or whatever if I hear anything or when we get it all set up. Thanks again for the coffee darling.

Tess smiled and gathered her things. She left quickly as though heading for the bus or train. Fiona immediately felt guilty for having possibly made her late. Eventually shaking the thought, she readied herself to start cleaning up and organizing for the end of the day. As she did so, the young man began closing his texts and said something to her in his trademark silent voice.

- Sorry? I couldn't hear you there again.

Fiona smiled as she spoke to him and he repeated himself awkwardly while checking to see if the other students in the department had heard their little conversation.

- I just said that you're much nicer than the other girl is.
- Well that's really sweet of you to say. But trust me, Tess is nice, too.

Fiona defended her new colleague as she was sure that Tess by no means meant harm had she dealt with this young guy with less of a smile than she did.

- Okay.
- Did you get plenty of work done today?

He paused and shuffled in his seat at the large desk while passing his eyes quickly over the collection of texts he had amassed in front of him.

- Yea… I guess. There's a lot of it that I don't understand, though.
- What program or degree are you doing?
- I'm in the second year of my PhD at the moment.

Fiona immediately thought that he looked way too young to be at that point of his academic career, but then there were stories of students entering grad studies and doctoral studies and crazy ages if they were smart enough for it. This guy certainly fit that bill.

The two talked while Fiona busied herself with the closing duties. She learned more about his program, but very little about him or indeed what it was he was actually studying at such a high level. He relaxed into the conversation somewhat as they spoke, and it seemed to help that Fiona kept her smile but very rarely looked at him while she was making the rounds.

- Well, I've got to close up now unfortunately. I can keep these texts aside for you if you plan to use them again tomorrow to save you some time.
- No that's fine. I finished most of them.

She glanced at the works he had been reading. When most students said they no longer needed whatever they had used, they would imply that they were "finished with it." It really sounded, though, like he actually meant he had read most of the texts from cover to cover.

- Okay then. Have a nice evening.
- Yea. You too. Fiona right?
- That's right.

Before she could ask his name in return he had smiled awkwardly and shuffled out amongst the other students that had overheard the end of the day warning. *Poor bastard is probably going to go home and try to find me on Facebook or something now.* It happened a lot to her and to her female friends. Apparently it was socially acceptable to find out as much information as you could about a person without actually asking for their information and then doing the rest on Facebook, thereby rendering the possibility of an awkward face-to-face rejection of any kind almost impossible. Fiona had stopped using it years ago. Jonathan had never had it and never really understood the appeal. They had both coasted off of their friends' use of such sites to keep informed about things. The walk home at the end of the day was cold and the air had begun to smell like autumn. The signs for Halloween sweets dominated even the smallest of corner shops on the walk and there would soon be pumpkins illuminating the few porches that could be seen from the sidewalk. For all her complaining about the cold, there was something beautiful about the fall and something even better about the clothes that she could wear during that time of year. She smiled to herself as she walked, knowing that Jonathan had been right when he said she would like it there if she decided to move there forever. His smell began to come back to the scarf that she wore to work. He had worn it for as long as she had known him, tucked carefully into his jacket or swept casually around his neck after a few drinks. *Yea. Still smells like him.*

---

18 - October 28th - Jonathan

His head was pounding when he woke up. Feeling the spot from which the pain radiated without opening his eyes, he quickly retracted his hand at the sharp pain he inadvertently caused. This was his first *drunk tank* visit since he was eighteen. His head was bruised where he had evidently fallen down the previous night while being detained. He remembered yelling in the street but the reason had left him. *Was Roob with me last night when I left the bar?* As he opened his eyes slowly he clocked where he was. The room had a similarly depressing vibe to the hospital building in which he had spent his time some months ago, only this room was much smaller and had very little inside it other than a silver toilet-bowl some four feet away from his head. Jon threw his head back against the thin mattress on which he'd slept and cursed quietly under his breath. His throat scratched with the hangover he would carry for at least the rest of the day. First things first: he assumed he had not done anything too bad, otherwise he would have been kept somewhere much worse or people would have been called and the situation would be more depressing than it already was. Fiona would undoubtedly be beyond pissed at him.

As the previous night had come to a close, Jonathan had snuck clear of Reuben, either on purpose or by accident, very quickly after the group left the bar. He remembered saying goodnight to Tom and Alex and watching them get into a taxi while he sat with his arse perched against a cold stone window ledge. He had held out a hand as his father did, opening and closing from palm to fist as a wave while their cab quietly pulled away. The rain had started by then. He brushed his hands over his jeans in the cell while he recollected and felt that they were still somewhat moist. *I must have been out in the rain for fucking ages. Or it must have rained really hard.* Reuben had also said goodbye to Karen at this point; he was sure of it, because she had not been there after the pub. Jon also still had a pint glass in hand some two hundred yards up the road from the pub they had just left. *That's when I lost Roob. I went back to give the glass back, he must have thought I was meeting him at the next place and needed cash or something from the machine.* Jon's phone was evidently in the possession if his jailer by the morning so he could not confirm any of his memories, and they returned to his mind with the sporadic and intermittent nature of a scratched record doing its absolute best to play its own version of "I'll Name that Tune."

After leaving Roob, Jon had managed a few more beers back in the same bar. Despite his slurred words and the numbness from the combination of painkillers he was on, he looked surprisingly sober and had no trouble getting served. In a university town you would rarely have an issue getting served if you looked over twenty-five anyway, regardless of what time it was. It was also the last place that Reuben would have gone to look for him. *Roob probably wouldn't have spent much effort on looking for me anyway. He's seen me way worse than that I think.* When the police cars made their rounds at the end of the night and cleared everyone out, Jon had apparently made a scene in the road, causing a random bystander to quickly knock him down, hence the pain in the back of his head the next morning. *That can't be why I'm in here though. . .*

While still contemplating his whereabouts from the previous night, an officer banged on his cell door and quickly entered with a form to sign and a clear plastic bag containing several of Jon's belongings. The metal clanging was enough to make Jon visibly wince and hold the sides of his head momentarily as he adjusted to the pain. They had apparently called Reuben to come and get him. Jon followed the officer carefully regarding him from behind through the haze of his hangover and headache. He smelled of something from his youth. *Brut, maybe Old spice, something like that.* The guy was really tall and stood a few inches above Jonathan who, at just over six feet, rarely felt dwarfed. The officer looked like he had once been in great shape but had recently turned muscle quickly into fat with several years of TV binges and very little exercise. *The police physical was a long time ago for this guy.* Without turning to face him as they walked down the hallway of the station, the officer was explaining that Jon had been found in the road after being punched, still holding a pint glass. They had returned the glass and Jon had fallen asleep against the police car in the process. It came down to public drunkenness, something for which Jon would receive no lasting punishment other than the physical pain he still felt as his head lolled with his steps while walking the hallway.

- Did you call my father, too?
- No.
- Why not? Reuben isn't related to me or anything.
- We aren't the hospital. We looked in your phone and your last 12 or so out going calls were to Mr. Crowell. Well, *Roob*, in your phone. You also made several calls to a "Fi" in your contact list, but none made it through.

The officer uttered Roob's name as if it had been something ridiculous and Jon immediately took offence. He hoped to see the officer's name tag and make a snappy retort about his name but his eyes could not focus on it when he managed to sneak quick glimpses. By the time they rounded the corner and saw Roob's hungover frame slumped in a chair in the same suit he had been wearing the night before, Jon forgot all about the nametag and looked into his friend's eyes across the room. Neither of the men were happy, but neither were sure if they should be upset with the other. *Whose fault was it all really?* Looking at the clock, Jon saw it was just after nine in the morning. Reuben could not have been asleep really any time before two the previous night, and as the two men walked wordlessly towards Jon's car in the parking lot, it crossed Jon's mind that Roob was probably still on the threshold of even being sober enough to drive by this point. *It's weird that the cop even let me get in a car with Roob…didn't even ask if he could… why the fuck did Roob bring my car?*

- Karen's got my car for work today. Geoff drove yours over for me when I told him what happened.

Roob had seemingly read Jon's mind when they got into the car. Jon was sure he was in no state to drive, and despite his hesitation, Roob looked slightly more up to the task as he had already managed to get himself there at least.

- Serious business mate, lending the car out already.

Roob was in no mood to bite. He let the comment slide knowing that Jon was looking for a rise. He was evidently still pissed.

The two men rode in silence back to Jon's place. Reuben followed his friend in through the front door and passed his eyes over the view before him. The place was actually pretty clean. Most things had not been moved out of the place they were left in from months before. Reuben assumed this was in some effort to keep Fiona around despite her absence. Jon had apparently not really noticed that his friend had come into his kitchen. He headed straight for the bathroom to take a shower without saying a word. Reuben wandered through the house and saw the various relics of the life that no longer existed outside of these walls. He was not sure if that life was only Fiona's or if Jon's was sliding along in a similar direction. Reuben meandered slowly through the weird museum of his friends' prior lives. His hands remained in his pockets throughout his little journey to prevent an accidental graze against something that was not to be moved. He looked quickly into Jon and Fiona's bedroom and saw the various discarded clothes left by Fiona from a night that, at first glance, could have been only a few days earlier. While nosing through the house, Reuben periodically listened for the sound of the water running to ensure he was still safe in his perusal. Jon would probably not be thrilled at his exploration. *Was all this stuff like this the last time I was here before Toni's wedding thing? Must have been.* Everything had been cleaned *around.* Jon's office was something of a different story. Aside from the unharmed stack of paper on the corner of the desk and the lack of blood, it looked like some sort of murder or crime scene had occurred from behind the desk.

Jon's papers were strewn across the floor and fluttered when Reuben opened the door. Various sheets possessed different stains and different evidence of incomplete work. A half-broken coffee mug contained a dark brown crust on the inside. It had clearly been there for a while, left unmoved like a terrible effort at contemporary artwork. *Probably the same crap he was having with his beer last night.* Several books rested awkwardly with pages crumpled, Reuben winced at the sight, his university days teaching him to respect books above all else. He bent down to pick up the coffee mug and set it on the table; he moved several papers aside revealing Jon's broken laptop beneath them.

- What are you doing?
- Oh, just working my way through your mess.

Jon was standing at the doorway to his office completely naked. A towel hung over his shoulder having just showered. Reuben answered without turning around and still regarding the broken laptop. In it's reflection he saw Jon and turned quickly to tell him to fuck off and get dressed.

- I should go mate. Give your dad a ring.
- Yea you should.

Reuben pushed passed his friend and left the apartment quickly. Jon thought about where he would go as he did not live close and had driven there using Jon's car. He had

110

evidently thought the interaction would have gone better and Jon would have taken him home.

Several rings had passed by the time Geoffrey picked up.

- You alright Jon?
- I'm fine. Roob dropped me off earlier this morning. It seemed worse than it was.
- What happened? Do you have to go to court or anything?

Surprisingly, Jon's father remained calm and was not judgemental throughout the phone call despite being worried about and disappointed with his son. Jon went through the motions of explaining what had happened the previous night and how it had led to him being put in the back of a police car before waking up on a sticky, plastic, two-inch-thick, wipeable mattress in the drunk tank. He explained that, having called the station to follow-up, he would be in no further trouble or anything at all. Geoff exhaled audibly through the phone and Jon held his own a few inches from his ear to mute the sound and seemingly avoid the breath in his ear. Jon had surprised himself by calling his dad as he had been told to do. He heard Fiona padding around the house while he held the phone away from his ear. His dad's breath in his ear over the phone reminded him of his reaction when he had called to say that he and Fiona had got married. Geoffrey may have been emotional on that occasion, but would have never admitted to such tears. It was unclear this time how Geoff was feeling from Jon's end of the phone. Difficult phone calls had been neither his nor Fiona's forte and he felt alone while waiting for his dad to respond; more alone somehow, than when he sat by himself with no phone call at all. He wanted Fiona to be sitting on his lap or making coffee so he could stand close behind her while he worked through whatever conversation raised his heart rate and accelerated his inevitable hair loss.

- Alright then. As long as you're ok mate.
- Yea. Sorry for worrying you guys. Mum there?
- No she's out at some class for something or other. I'll tell her you asked to speak to her, though.
- She pissed?
- Yea, but glad you're alright.

Geoff hung up after a short pause and Jon stood in his kitchen for a while without saying too much. Neither father nor son had acknowledged the bigger issue about Jon's mishap the night before. He had expected to be grilled about why he had got so drunk, what he was thinking, or what other people would think of it. He quickly realized that such questions would have usually come from Fiona rather than anyone else. Geoff knew and understood that his son was a grown man. Not too much of what he could say would have a great deal of impact should it come from him. Clara would obviously be worried about him, but likely would not dare to ask too many questions should she upset anyone. Jon looked down the hall at his office. *I really need to clean that shit up.*

---

19 - November 20th – Fiona

Tess had come over several times since they'd first met at work. Fiona looked around in her little apartment at the pictures of Jonathan while she drank wine with her small circle of friends. Alex had left Tom at home this time as she had come straight from the university and he would join later from whatever work he was finishing up at home, but surprisingly Reuben had made an appearance despite Jonathan's obvious absence. He was seeing some new girl named Karen who was one of Tess's friends before they had all met. Fiona felt uncomfortable. This was a new house. There were new friends there. Reuben was there. Jonathan was not. *Were we friends? They were.* Looking at his pictures only cemented the knowledge in her already tired mind that he was not coming back and that things were changing all around her. Her friends momentarily irritated her as they were masking whatever was left of Jonathan in her apartment. She missed him like crazy. Her little notebook and fountain pen lay just beyond arms reach behind the bottle of wine through which she had been quietly working. She had tried writing to him on its small blank pages but it had felt forced. It was best to stop drinking. Her glass had been empty for about twenty minutes and, after pouring for her friends, Fiona headed to the kitchen to make tea instead.

It had been a point of pride for herself and Jonathan over the time they had been together. Despite obvious fun nights out and obligatory special occasions, the two had always maintained a relatively simple and safe drinking routine. It had seemed like much more fun to the both of them to be coherent upon arriving home so that they could actually pass the evening having sex rather than spinning at a standstill between the sheets and being scared to open or close their eyes. They enjoyed drinking, but enjoyed each other much more. Two years earlier she had been shown how lucky she was.

- Does Jonathan ever get like that?
- Like what sorry?

She had been spaced out during the conversation.

- So drunk that he doesn't come home or is just a total mess when he does.
- No, not really.

Her friend had been retelling the story of her boyfriend who had apparently made a habit of drinking past the point of no return and relying on her to clean up his mess. Fi felt bad for living on the safe side of the conversation and undoubtedly making her friend feel worse for her boyfriend's behaviour, but not bad enough to wish anything was different for herself and Jonathan. She felt as though she had high-roaded a friend who had attempted to be funny with a racist or sexist joke by saying something like "oh… well I don't look at the world that way." The truth was, most of the time they went out drinking or socializing, it would be together, or they would drive anyway. She wondered quietly if that made her sad or codependent. Her thoughts were cut short as she snapped back to her new living room and her new friends. Her tea was doing wonders for her mood. She felt Jonathan's hand on the back of her neck playing with her hair while the group talked. He was gone, but he was always there when she needed him. Alex passed Fiona a tissue while still talking about something to do with her dissertation with Karen and Reuben. Apparently a few tears had been making their way down her face without her realizing. Only Alex had noticed; she was just as in tune with the sporadic calendar of Fiona's crying by this point and was by no means someone to judge.

Fiona smiled and curled her legs up on to the couch beneath her. Everyone would likely make their way home soon enough, leaving her to go to sleep alone. She would certainly be avoiding the spins and the drowning in remnants of the evening's alcohol like many others would be. *Reuben is drinking less; he looks really happy.* He was sitting in his usual uncomfortable posture on the couch, but it looked somehow more natural with Karen sharing his spot. Sitting back and clutching her tea, Fiona studied the two of them carefully while listening absently to the conversation at hand. It was getting depressing again because the topic had shifted back to more global conflict, presidential races in some such place, or some natural disaster that required attention as it had stolen countless lives. Karen was mirroring Fi as she spoke very little. She had one hand gently pressed on Reuben's leg. It was still blowing Fi's mind to see Reuben in such a state, but it was more confusing to see it coming so naturally to the pair of them. She was much shorter than him and her heels waited for her by the front door. Despite the cold, she had worn a dress out to the little gathering. *I guess it has only been a few months for them. Still honeymoon phase. Still trying to impress each other.* It worked for them both. Her legs were folded beneath her and she leant gently towards Reuben; the expression she wore perhaps suggested a sense of caution as she did. It would be awful if she scared him off, but she still wanted to be near him.

Jonathan would have liked her. He would have liked to see Reuben happy. There had been a change in their dynamic since Fi and Jon had got married. While not really tangible or worth bringing up, Jonathan had noticed it and so had Fi. She felt bad watching him sit with Karen while Jonathan couldn't be a part of it. Every few seconds Karen would tuck her hair behind her ears and readjust to the conversation from behind her black-framed glasses. Despite the trend of people wearing them with either clear lenses or no lenses at all, it seemed like she needed them a little as she refocused momentarily upon shifting her gaze around the room. She was out of character for Reuben, but upon thinking it, Fi retracted her initial perspective and realized she would not have really known what would have been *in* character for him. Karen was pretty, she seemed intelligent, and generally seemed to have a positive impact on Reuben. *That's kind of the whole point really isn't it?*

Fiona returned to the conversation to find that things had become much more lighthearted since her last check.

- Yea but we should really be getting the opinion of the youths among us right?

It was something Tom said fairly often. Despite only being twenty-four, and by no means the oldest person in attendance, Tom frequently made jokes about his age. It was something he had in common with Jon, but Jon had the early signs of hair loss to back it up.

- What? That's not fair! You'll all judge me now, though.

Tess, at twenty-two, was evidently the "youth" upon whom Tom was calling. Her music taste was being called into question. Several justifications and loud bursts of laughter from the group later, it seemed as though she had passed the relative test. Soon after, everyone began to shuffle towards the door, hug Fiona, and say goodbyes. Tess stayed after a short while to help Fiona clean. She was awkward about Jonathan but could avoid the conversation easily because she had never known him. She looked carefully at several of the pictures of he and Fiona that were proudly displayed around the little flat. There was something that had changed in Fiona's face since they were taken. It was more than simply time passing. Tess had spent her teen years watching her father battle cancer. He had been lucky in the end. There was nothing left to suggest that he had even fought for so long other than what Tess saw in his face. She could see the difference. What had been a confident smile in his youth that had endured any and all hardships, had long been worn down; its corners rested a little lower on his face despite the effort, as though the muscles were simply too tired to lift it to its former height and glory. Fiona's face bore a similar strain.

20 - November 30th - Fiona

It was an odd feeling to wake up on the morning of Jonathan's birthday only for him not to be there. He had not been one to celebrate birthdays religiously by any means, and they had only been together for three of them so far anyway, but it had been strange to know that the *day* was looming. Time had built up towards the thirtieth and then the day had arrived and the coffee was on in the kitchen in the morning as usual while Fiona meandered around her apartment half-dressed getting ready for work. Nobody at work would know that it had been Jonathan's birthday, nor would they care. Jonathan had been of the mindset that after you turn eighteen, the only big ones are twenty, twenty-one, thirty, forty, and so on from there. It looked cold outside but relatively sunny with very little breeze when Fi looked out of her little kitchen window. She passed her hands through her hair; it was getting longer than it had been since she first started dating Jonathan. *Looks like a nice day outside. No red sky this morning.*

He would be twenty-six. She would not turn twenty-eight until April, so for half the year her power of dominion over him that she was granted by her age was sliced in half numerically. She laughed to herself on her way to work, opting for her travel mug of coffee over the unnecessary umbrella.

- Hey babe how're you doing today?

Alex showed up just minutes after Fi had opened up the department. The din of the lights still seemed to be making their way up to their full luminescence as Alex dumped her bag and sat cross-legged on the long desk. She reached back for her coffee and took a loud sip while Fiona kept herself busy.

- Yea I'm alright darling. Just the usual, you know.
- He'd be 26 today, right?
- How do you always remember everyone's birthday?
- Well, for one I'm awesome. But mostly it's because we live in the smartphone era. Tom and I both got notifications this morning. Being a dick and forgetting someone's birthday pretty much has to be on purpose these days.

Both women laughed at the sentiment. Even Jon and Fi, who were relatively invisible digitally, were apparently not immune to internet searches

- Unless you're Jonathan I guess. I swear he would still use a "brick phone" if it was socially acceptable.
- Yea you're right. I think Tom hates the whole online deal too, though. I think they are both just silently turning into reluctant hipsters.

It felt nice for Fiona to be able to talk about Jonathan without glorifying him at every turn. He was not perfect, but he seemed to be for her. They had been together long enough to know that perfection seldom exists on it's own in someone's partner; rather, it had to be found or looked for by someone who was willing to do so. This was why it still felt good to be able to mock Jonathan's old-man-ness when he was not there. It was something he knew she did with Alex frequently anyway, so why should it change just because he had gone?

- Are you going to get your application done babe?

Fi groaned and exhaled hard. She had hardly been too busy to take on the task, and it was something she had always wanted to do.

- I should, eh?

- Absolutely. If you do it here you have plenty of time to get it done, but if you go overseas, which you can't because I would kill you, then you have no time at all.
- So?
- So, what I'm saying is, yes you have plenty of time. No you're not allowed to go overseas and leave me to deal with Tom and Reuben every day by myself, and yes, you should do your application sooner rather than later anyway because it's exciting.

It *was* exciting. Jonathan would be proud of her if she did. She chatted with Alex for a long time, definitely neglecting her work, about proposals and ideas for her PhD topic. It was something she had been working on silently in her head ever since completing her undergraduate degree. Although her field was very different to Alex's, she felt better talking about it out loud and was comfortable with the criticism and help that she offered. *Alex is a damn genius; if I do this it will definitely be worth it to do it here. I wouldn't want to leave her anyway because that would be awful, but she could help so much with my work.*

Alex had a clarity about the way she spoke which, when talking about anything academic, made things shockingly easy to understand. She would be published and republished throughout her career if she chose to stay in academia. When talking about things unrelated to her work, such clarity sometimes appeared blunt and often made for some entertaining first impressions with new people in groups. It was a quality in herself of which she was very aware and had absolutely no intention of changing whatsoever.

- Yea. Well, we will get it done this week. Like, we can get it started at least. We'll have it done before Christmas.

After Alex had finished whatever she needed to do for the day, she headed out and left Fiona to the quiet seclusion of the Special Collections department. There were no students and no laptops or books that had been left out suggesting that anyone would be back anytime soon. Fiona mused to herself as to why things might be so empty. It was possibly due to the fact that the exam season was just around the corner for undergraduate and master's students. Whatever they would have needed to research for exams would probably need to have been researched and finished long before this point or it would just be too late. That being said, there were always PhD students like Alex, or people who had left things until the very last minute. Fi leant back in her chair and enjoyed the privacy she had at work. There was a spot between the two largest bookshelves, used for holding the heavy and bulky journal folders, that was unseen by the security cameras. When she had first noticed this feature, that particular spot had been Fiona's favourite place to send a sneaky text or check emails while she was at work. After realizing, some time later, that she was the only person who would generally see whatever footage happened in her department unless something untoward occurred, she resumed texting at her desk without worry. She wasn't lazy or careless about her work, and always made sure things were done as well as they could be, but a quick text never hurt anyone. Fi checked her screen to see if there were any waiting; it had been so long since Jonathan's name had appeared on her screen in such a way. Thankfully, though, she'd stopped texting him out of instinct or by accident.

The distinctive shuffle of the windbreaker broke the silence and Fiona called a friendly hello from her desk.

-   Need the usual stuff today?

- Yes. I'm still really busy. Everyone else seems to just be prepping for exams now, my deadlines are coming up just after Christmas.

This was perhaps the longest answer she had ever heard from the young guy. Without meaning to, she didn't really take notice of what he had said after hearing that he needed the same books as on his previous visit. She had switched to work-mode and started to find the specific texts. On her way, she grabbed several books and files that were still laying around so that she could reorganize their contents at her desk.

- How are you today? Is your friend Alex coming?

Fiona turned and backed out of the aisle between the shelves carrying a large stack of texts and faced the young man. *How does he know Alex? I guess he met her that first time, must have heard her name. Crazy memory, this kid.*

- No, well. She was already here this morning so I doubt she will be back today.

He paused and seemed to relax a little while tracing invisible shapes with his index finger on the big table and looking down.

- Okay then. I really do have lots to do.

Well, that was like fifty unsolicited words from the poor guy. He's on a roll today. Fiona handed him the texts he needed, went back to her desk with her pile of disorganization, and began tidying things up. It was ridiculous to Fiona how people could use some of these journals, most of which were old and valuable, and leave them in such a state. She gently passed her hands over a hardback bound edition of the second volume of a literary journal from 1914 called *The Egoist*. Whoever had previously used the text had felt the need to mark out their work in pencil in the margins as they went along. Fiona gently erased each of the markings surrounding a part of the early serialized publication of James Joyce's *A Portrait of the Artist as a Young Man*.

It was coincidental that this text happened to be one of her favourites. A gift she had given to Jonathan on his twenty-fourth birthday had been a collection of photos she had gathered of him in different situations. There was "A Portrait of the Artist as a Tired Man" as he slept on the couch. "A Portrait of the Artist as a Bruised Man" from some hospital visit or another followed among a collection of several more.

Fiona used the "snake-weights" to hold the pages down while standing the large book on a sturdy book-rest while she did her work. *Always sounds like shake-weight.* She laughed to herself while moving the little white, sand-filled bags gently to the edges of the pages each time she changed her place. While musing over the *Portrait* references she thought to herself that an excellent addition to the collection would have been a pre-Karen edition of Reuben entitled *A Portrait of the Artist as a Drunk Man,* as just about everyone in their circle of friends could produce a picture of Roob looking drunk or bewildered on their phone at any given time. Karen seemed to be bringing out the best in him.

- I'm really sorry about your husband.

Fiona barely heard the little voice behind her as usual.

- Excuse me?
- I said I'm really sorry about your husband.

She was quickly taken aback and was unsure about how to respond. *How does this guy know about Jonathan? There's no way he actually knew him.*

- Um… Thankyou. How did you know about Jonathan if you don't mind me asking?

The little man looked worried, as though he had offended Fiona deeply.

- I'm sorry. I just heard you talking last time with your friend. Your friend Alex. About your husband.

He was being kind and Fiona was scaring the hell out of the guy as she was unable to react appropriately.

- Oh. Thanks. That's really nice of you.

Without thinking about it properly and letting her mouth decide how to continue the conversation, Fiona continued her awkward interaction.

- I miss him lots, but it's all Okay. Do you have a girlfriend or a wife?

She winced at her own question. She felt bad for putting the guy on the spot. It was none of her business what this guy's relationship situation was and she didn't even care anyway. All the same, they were in the midst of the conversation now so it was happening whether she liked it or not.

- No. No. I don't. I did, but I don't now.
- Oh, Okay.

It was awkward. *What the fuck do I say? Is that the kind of answer that I am supposed to say sorry to? I need more information to know if I am supposed to feel bad for the guy. Fuck, I want this conversation to be over.* She needed some sort of exit. The subject needed to be changed. The amount of time since either of them had said anything was stretching on now and the awkwardness was tangible. Jonathan would, by this point have managed to find a reason to leave politely, casually shooting any adjacent party a glance back towards the odd nature of the prior situation. Alex would have commented on the awkwardness and left. Reuben would have out-awkwarded the young guy and the world may have ended entirely.

- Yea. It's fine, though.
- That's good to hear. Do you need any help with anything else?
- No. Thanks.

He shuffled off and she exhaled audibly. *I guess it's progress that I didn't cry in front of him or anything.* She pressed the button on her phone, looked at Jonathan's picture and smiled. She heard the windbreaker shuffle as the guy stacked his books on the desk neatly and headed out the door without saying goodbye. Had it been anyone else, Fiona would have been sure that she had offended them or that they were unhappy with her.

---

21 - Jonathan – November 30th

Surprisingly, Jon remembered his own birthday. Still wallowing, any marker or specific moment in the calendar served only as a reminder of previous years or previous points in his life at which he was apparently happier or more fortunate. It had been about a month since his brief overnight vacation in the drunk-tank. The cracked screen of his phone illuminated itself periodically as he stretched and kicked in his bed in the morning. He had nowhere that he needed to be and he saw between the cracks in the screen of his phone that he had slept in until just before eleven in the morning. *Well today's going to be fucking interesting.* Still enjoying the semi-conscious state provided by the previous night's sleep, he stretched his arm out to the empty side of the bed. *Fiona must already be up by now.* Wiping his eyes roughly he slid his back up against the headboard and rotated his pillow behind him. The room was still fairly dark as his curtains worked hard to keep out the bright sunshine that would otherwise pour in and bring the space kicking and screaming into the new day. A bright square outline of light peeked though at the edges of the curtains' domain.

Jon quickly knew he was alone. The usual signs of pain in his body and the familiar feeling of drowning in his own head returned as he stretched out of bed to start his day.

What was that? Four seconds of blissful ignorance? His curtains stayed closed as he shuffled down the hallway, leaving his phone vibrating on the little table beside his bed. Over the past few weeks he had changed his outlook somewhat. The rooms of his house, while maintaining a shrine-like quality towards Fiona, were much more organized and clean. The mountain of papers atop his broken laptop in his office had been discarded and the laptop lay closed on his now dust-free desk. The swivel-chair behind it was no longer functioning as overflow from his closest and carried no clothes as it once had. Natural light flooded into the previously dark room and illuminated the wood of the desk and the many books lining the walls. Shafts of light still pointed out the dust in the air. He could almost feel it in his throat after seeing it so clearly. It was the office he had wanted when he was a younger man. It was missing the pipe and the bar enclosed within an antique-looking globe, but it also was not 1935 and he was not Indiana Jones. He had a respectable work-space. A new laptop would certainly not go amiss, though.

From the kitchen Jon could hear his phone inching its way around the free space on his bedside counter. It occasionally rattled up close to something that sounded metal; probably his keys or some loose changed that he'd left there. He had no intention of answering it just yet. The day before, he had texted his father to invite him for lunch. It was worth it to get ahead of the onslaught that would otherwise occur. This meant that he only had a few hours, as Geoff would be over with Clara around one-thirty in the afternoon, to do what he really wanted to. The kitchen was spotless as he seldom cooked in it of late. The coffee that Fiona had bought still resided in the can on the side and Jon had bought his own coffee that stayed in the cupboard with a spoon permanently poking from the top of its packaging. All of her things were now organized the way she would have liked them. His bedroom, their bedroom, while currently stifled of light, spent the day welcoming the sunlight over the articles of clothing which had now acquired their own specific places. No longer did Fiona's lingerie and clothing hang from the furniture in complete disarray. Her scarves hung from the mirror, as it was now the "scarf area." The closet, still containing predominantly Fiona's clothing aside from the few things that Alex had come by to collect while Jon had supervised carefully, was now perfectly organized into different areas. Her summer clothes occupied one side as the trend shifted towards heavier and longer clothes for winter as it got nearer to the corner of the room which was further out of reach. Her many pairs of shoes obviously lined the foot of the closet, with belts and bags resting just behind them. She had clothes and shoes he was sure she had never worn in the time that he had known her, but he knew all of her things well.

It was not the first time he had spent his weekend organizing Fiona's wardrobe for her.

- I don't get it babe.

He scratched his head in frustration and confusion while staring into the abyss of the closet, his feet nestled between several days' worth of discarded clothes that were "not dirty so she couldn't put them in the wash yet, but also not clean so she couldn't hang them back up either or she would forget what she had already worn and lose track." Jon knew this was bullshit and she would eventually have stepped on things enough times that they would be deemed "dirty" enough to go into the wash, at which point Jon would scoop them all up and take them through to the laundry room.

- What don't you get darling?

- How are you so clean and tidy and organized with, like, every other part of your life, but your clothes are just a bloody nightmare?

He was laughing as he scratched his head.

- I mean, your *job* is *literally* in organization.
- I know, but it's organized to me.

She smiled innocently. She *did* have a system of sorts, but it was more out of habit that she stuck to it than because it actually worked.

- Okay... Well. Your *organization* aside, would you be pissed if I organized it?
- I'm certainly not going to be pissed if you are volunteering to take it on.

She laughed, knowing that he would do it for her. It was clearly frustrating him far too much to leave it the way it was.

His — her — closet had stayed clean for much longer this second time around. She had yet to re-tarnish the organizational schematic or disrupt the order that Jon had asserted over the prior madness. He missed the madness now and seldom opened the door to her half of the closet, opting instead to reach for things without looking too closely when he needed them. His bathroom now displayed the many bottles of different makeups, hair products, face creams, and whatever else Fiona had paid obscene amounts for in a well organized display around the sink. Jon was able to lift and move things in order to clean around them. He had justified this step based on Fiona's reaction several years earlier when he had offered to clean the closet. It was just him being useful. It was a purpose that he'd lost in recent months; he could, once again, do things for her. The towel that had once been pressed into the corner of the bathroom tiling on the counter was now cleaned and folded in the same place. The shower floor was now free of used razors that had been a plague of prior months and years; it had been more than once that Jon had stepped on one of Fiona's discarded razor handles and found new ways to utter profanity through the steam. All such chagrin had been masked under the noise of the shower head and the whirr of the fan in the bathroom.

Jon had even cleaned himself up somewhat. The gaunt expression that usually walked alongside bereavement had not yet left him, and he had certainly lost weight, but he looked much more put-together since his little spell on the police mattress. His hair had lost the Reuben-style it was beginning to work towards. His beard had also reacquired the perpetual but organized visible length to which Fiona had grown accustomed during their marriage. After brushing his teeth and actually flossing, something he had done maybe seven times in the previous decade, he went back to his bedroom and dressed in a semi-formal blue shirt with some black jeans and clean, dark grey shoes. He threw a jacket around himself and walked to the car to head to go for a drive before his day changed entirely and his parents arrived. *It's going to be a long day. Wouldn't surprise me if they drag along Roob and whatsername or Tom and Alex or something. Karen. Her name is Karen, don't be a cock.*

It was comfortable behind the wheel. The car had the same ticks as the one that had almost killed him. Each gear responded in the same way, the pedals stuck to the balls of his feet with a familiarity that comforted him greatly. He drove for over an hour and did not flinch when he passed the spot where the old car had flipped. The fact that it was even the same road had not even crossed his mind until several hundred yards before the exact spot. He turned his head to focus his eyes on the spot for a few fractions of a second longer than he would have had it been just another spot of tarmac on his journey. Any evidence that something so serious had occurred there had long disappeared by now. A cross with flowers that had been lain by several passers by who had read the news story and had been added to by Fiona's friends was also no longer resting beside the road. The radio was on. The well spoken, posh-accented BBC news reporter explained the cause of the attacks that were *still* occurring as though it was meant to affect people in any lasting sort of way. The people had still died, and many more would evidently do so. The problems in the area had been ongoing for many years and would continue even with radical change, it seemed inevitable that things just went on; everything did.

Despite the knowledge of the world still turning provided by the news on the radio, the familiarity of the story soothed Jon's aching memory and continued to revert him somewhat back to a prior time. Things could move on and stay the same at the same time. Fiona was still singing at home; she just didn't want to go where he was going today. *I don't even want to go where I'm going today.* His shoes crunched on the white gravel of the parking lot when he arrived and swung his legs out of the door. There was a serenity washing over the area that he had not expected to radiate out this far away from the headstones themselves. Two or three cars were already present in the parking lot, none of which he recognized. A younger looking man than he would have expected to see at the cemetery sat visibly sobbing behind the wheel of his car. This was strange. The man was in his early thirties at best. *What had happened to him to be here? Who was he missing? He's just about too young to have logically lost his parents.*

Walking on and still crunching the white gravel, the parking lot narrowed to a path that led towards the headstones. Jon realized that he was easily more than five years younger than the crying man. He still did not understand his own situation. It was as alien to him as it was to everyone who pretended to understand and help him deal with the loss of the biggest part of him that he could lose while staying alive himself; if only just.

- Well. I don't know why she is going to be buried there in Scotland to be honest Jonathan.

Fiona's mother was trying to be polite and calm about the situation, but was hurt that Fiona would not be going back to Portland to be buried.

- Her life is here Kathy. Was here...

He paused and tried to find the words. As it had been less than a week since she had died, neither was able to talk properly about it.

- What I'm trying to say is, we were going to live here for the foreseeable future. It was in neither of our plans or visions of the future to end up back in the states. At least that's how I understood things. Her friends are her, her life.

Kathy had, surprisingly, taken the news well that her daughter would be buried overseas after what was just a short back and forth with her son-in-law. By the time a mother had to deal with burying her child, arguing over the location in such a way seemed pointless and irrelevant. She reconciled herself with her Fi's funeral arrangements quickly and had joined Jon at the service several days later.

Standing in front of Fi's small, grey headstone, Jon thought about Kathy and the last time the two had been stood together in the same spot. He had, surprisingly, kept in frequent contact with her above almost everyone else since then. She was non-intrusive. She was hurting in the same way that he was, and she dealt with things in the same way that he did without being nearby enough to interfere with his life or his questionable coping mechanisms. He doubted that Geoff and Clara knew that he had been talking with Kathy more than with them. They would be upset, but would probably understand. The sun was brightening the sky, but only through a thick layer of white clouds. It was a day when sunglasses were undoubtedly necessary, but it still felt gloomy outside. Had trees not lined the small field of body-allotments, the edge of the grass would have met the white of the sky with a curve that felt infinite. Everything about the light was flat. Kathy knew he would be seeing Fi today. She had not sent him a message. He was grateful for it. It was nice to be alone with her and away from her singing in the apartment. He missed the sound, but it was becoming less and less real with each moment he spent in its company.

Jon passed his hand slowly over his face where his beard grew close and knelt into a crouch on the balls of his feet. The grass was still wet and left its marks on his shoes like abstract paintbrush strokes. The wind masked most of the noise from the adjoining road and added to the sense of seclusion. The field undulated enough to conceal many of the other visitors. It was not the weekend and it was daytime, so there were few people present to shatter the illusion, and none within earshot of Fiona and Jonathan. The words on the headstone resonated with Jon deeply. He had chosen them in a haste of sadness and exhaustion in the days that followed her death. *She would like them, for sure.* His left hand was resting on top of the cold stone above where her name was etched. There were spots of water forming around his hand as it started to rain. Feeling the spots touch his head and hearing them spatter against his jacket he realized how long he had been sat motionless at Fiona's feet. Still in his crouch position, his legs had disappeared from beneath him and strained to come back to life as he realized their absence and slowly began to stand again.

Noiselessly under the now greying sky, Jon walked back to the path and began his trudge back towards the car. He had said and thought all that he needed to. His feet made the familiar crunch as they rejoined the path and the parking lot. He clicked into his seatbelt and drove away slowly, preparing internally for the afternoon that would follow.

---

22 - Jonathan – November 30th

Roob's car waited in the driveway as he pulled up behind it. *That'll be annoying later. We'll all have to move our cars in some ridiculous order when people leave.* The driveway was narrow and straight; in recent months the moss had begun to creep through the crevices between the brickwork. What could have looked like neglect instead seemed welcoming, as though the cold weather still made some effort to see things grow. There was space enough for three cars, one behind the other, and further space on the street for anyone else. It foolishly crossed Jon's mind that he had not offered Fi a lift home from work and she would be needing a ride. This would make it useful that he was at the back of the line. *She doesn't need a ride, idiot.* Geoff's car waited in front of Roob's. No passengers sat in either vehicle. *Oh no, that's fine, just let yourselves in. Jon won't mind at all.* His mum waved through the kitchen window as he walked up the driveway past the cars. She was washing dishes that he had already washed. He knew he had left the kitchen with nothing for her to do and that would be killing her so she had evidently taken it upon herself to correct his workmanship. She smiled; he returned the gesture as well as

132

he could and walked in. Roob had put the TV on in the living room while Karen filtered back and forth from there to the kitchen where Jon's parents were making cups of tea. It was nice. It just wasn't Jon's house when this was happening. *Would Fiona like this?* He winced as he could not work it out. *Was this something she would have enjoyed? I don't know really anymore.*

It was, for Jon, a surprisingly painless afternoon as it went along. Despite having been initially worried about Karen's presence as it changed his idea of Reuben, she became useful in the conversation as the five of them talked and had tea in the living room. Jon lay on the ground by the coffee table while Roob and Karen shared the small couch. Geoff and Clara had the armchairs. It felt as though everyone was staring down at Jon while he nursed his tea.

- Are you sure your back is alright laying like that darling?

Clara's concern was legitimate but she knew that even if he was hurting he would not make anyone move. When she spoke with concern about her son, her face pursed and aged. In the three years that had passed since he had known Fiona, his parents seemed to have added ten years to their faces and strides.

- I'm fine. How are you guys? It's been a little while since we have spent much time together, eh? Especially here.
- That's 'cause you've been such an elusive bastard in recent weeks mate.

Roob's direct nature obviously had not changed as a result of Karen's presence.

- Yea. You're right, mate. but you'd be too busy anyway now that you're all loved up, eh?

Jon's parents chimed in with intrigue and began asking all of the necessary questions about Karen and Roob and how they

133

met. It was comfortable. Despite being an odd conversation for Jon, because it was so strange for Roob to be in such a relationship, Jon's parents grilling Roob for information and being confused by the answers was comforting and familiar. *They're here for my birthday. They came over to make sure I was okay.* Jon stared upwards at the conversation from behind a cup of tea. His nods and quiet mumblings of agreement were enough to keep him involved. Despite him being the reason this small group had assembled, he was irrelevant to it all. There had been a distance opening between himself and his family; even more so between himself and the friends he had known for years. This space quickly made him anxious. His arm was falling asleep beneath his weight as he had been laying propped up on one elbow and forearm on the carpet for quite some time. It was as though his body knew that parts of him were actually beginning to disappear or fade out. He shuffled away from his spot and felt the blood rush back to his arm as though releasing a swarm of tiny pinpricks into his fingertips. The carpet was warm to the touch and was depressed beneath his weight throughout the afternoon. He momentarily accepted his place as a part of the furniture. True to form, he had been sweating through his shirt beneath his arms unknowingly despite the relative cool of the living room. The map of scar tissue on his back clung desperately to the fabric of his shirt as he sat up and pretended to keep listening.

Karen dealt well with the barrage of questioning. It soon abated as Roob had begun to explain more of his work to Jon's parents.

- You've been really busy with work though recently haven't you, mate?

The question caught Jon by surprise for several reasons. He had been spaced out while nodding along for quite some time; focusing much more on the sky outside and absently moving his head while feeling the sensation return to his hands and his lower back with each shift of position. More importantly, he had no good answer to what should have been a simple question.

- What?
- Work, mate. How's it all going? We never see you because you're so damn busy all the time.

The colour of the sky had changed outside with the question, casting a new lens across the room, and Jon was forced back into the present entirely. What was beyond the window was purely out of reach and it was his turn to be present.

- Actually, no.

Jon spoke calmly and looked at Reuben directly as he did.

- What do you mean, you've just been avoiding us then, eh?

Reuben made light of Jon's strange answer but was still confused by what was happening.

- He's all caught up, right Jon?

Clara had joined in to defend her son without a shred of knowledge or evidence about his situation. The gesture came from a place of compassion but lacked legitimacy, understanding, or any sense of depth, and was therefore completely useless. The effort fell on deaf ears and Geoff leant forwards and tried to extrapolate more from Jon, who was evidently not volunteering more information of his own accord.

- What are you talking about Jon? We thought you had been really busy these past few months with work. It's all you've been doing…

His voice trailed off as Jon slowly opened his mouth to begin answering.

- I got sacked actually, Dad.

135

Jon was glad he was sitting up by the time he had shared his "news." The feeling of being looked down upon was mitigated a little bit as he was higher up than he had been before. Nobody spoke for a little while as there wasn't really a correct response or question. Geoff clearly wanted to know why. He widened his eyes as he stared at Jon, who stared back calmly and with a vacant expression.

- I need the bathroom, I'll be back, hang on.

Jon got up and groaned at the pain in his back and hands before quietly sidling out of the room with everyone else staring at him. *Well, that will give them something to talk about while I am out of the room for a bit I'm sure.*

Jon left his tea on the kitchen counter and walked to the bathroom. There were various murmurings coming from the living room in his absence. He had no intention of going into any further details when he returned, but there was no point in being dishonest with his family and friends about what he was doing with his time.

- Why did they sack you?

Jon was fifteen when he was *let go* from his job at the sport shop. He had worked maybe fifteen shifts over the course of several months and spent every penny of the few pounds an hour that the position had offered. The job had been fun and he was good at it. Stacking boxes and following basic instructions was hardly rocket science, even for a teenager. As he was only fifteen at the time, he was not really supposed to be allowed to work for another year, so he was paid cash and rarely had to interact with any customers. It was the easiest sort of job for a kid of his age. The truth was that he had just stopped wanting to be there. Sometimes the reasons for something coming to an end were as simple as that.

- I didn't go to work last week and I never called them to let them know that I wouldn't be there.
- Oh, I'm sure they will give you your job back if you go in and say you're sorry, darling.

Jon's mum was ready to march down to the shop with him and make some impassioned speech to the owner about how Jon was a good boy, and how he really loved his job and had not made any mistakes other than this one. She would say that she would talk to him at home and make sure that she checked his work schedule for him.

- I don't want to work there anymore though, mum.

She paused for a moment and stopped readying her purse for the outing she was already preparing in her mind.

- Oh. Okay. If you are sure darling.
- I am. It was fun for a bit, but I just don't like going to work there and it isn't worth it for the money.

There was very little that Jon's parents could say in response. Most fifteen-year-olds were not so sure of their position or sure about what they wanted. It seemed, however, from Jon's stern expression that this was something he had thought through and made a conscious decision about for himself. Despite the pride that Geoff felt towards his son for making such a choice, he still had to discipline him a little about not calling in before planning on taking a day off by himself. It was a lesson that Jon learned quickly and did not repeat.

By the time Jon had returned from the bathroom and collected his tea on the way, the conversation had reached an audible level. Once again, it was about him but did not include him just yet. He sat down carefully on the floor so as to not strain his wrists and the chatter stopped.

- Sorry to hear that you've not been working, mate.

It was not the response he had expected. At twenty-six, Jon still felt as though his parents would scold him like a child or treat him like he had misbehaved when things in his life did not go according to some sort of heavily thought out plan.

- Thanks Dad. I'll sort something out. You know me.
- Okay.

As if things had never reached any point of awkwardness, the conversation moved on and Jon's newly unemployed status was not mentioned for the rest of the afternoon. *Are they just being weird because they don't want to fuck up my "birthday afternoon?" Is it because Roob and Karen are here?* He'd expected a different reaction; a little more pomp and circumstance, perhaps. Jon settled back into the positional shifting on the carpet while the group chatted; it was a conversation of which he had actually become a part. He enjoyed talking with his parents, despite being confused about their earlier response. Fiona was singing loudly in the bedroom, he could not wait to go to bed and close his eyes while laying next to her. Her name was ominously vacant from the living room discussion, but consistently pulsed through his body in synchrony with his heartbeat. It was comforting to know that she was still there.

It had felt like a longer afternoon than it really was by the time Jon looked at his watch after the second cup of tea. Six o'clock was nearing and he had things to do, he was sure of it. What the things were remained unclear, but there was an urgency within him that compelled him to *get things done* so that he could relax later in the evening. His family left at the same time as Roob and Karen. Jon pulled his car all the way up the driveway and sat in the driver's seat amongst the newly forming moss beneath the car and contemplated his afternoon. The sun had disappeared some time earlier and a gloom had descended over the area. As he removed the keys and opened the door to the car, the lights automatically flicked on and shone his reflection back to him in the rear-view mirror. Among the plethora of things that were busying Jon's mind, the sight of Fiona asleep in the passenger's seat remained the most stark and clear behind his eyes. His own reflection worried him as he had indeed aged more significantly in the months that had followed her death. She was still perfect in his mind, despite the blurring and pixilation of the backgrounds in which he envisioned her. The memories were becoming less clear and markedly more opaque despite his everyday visits to their domain.

---

23 - Fiona – December 10th

Fiona had made the decision to go to Portland for the Christmas period. Kathy would be happy. Geoff and Clara would be alright with David at home, and things would be different enough in Portland that an otherwise impossible experience to deal with might actually go by without breaking her apart inside. The cracks were there; she could feel them. It was an act of self-preservation to remove herself from everything for a few weeks and prevent them from really opening up and letting everything terrible flood out.

- Are you sure you don't mind covering for me on either side of the Christmas break? I don't want it to get in the way of any work you have to do or exams or whatever.
- No no, it's totally fine. I could really use the money around Christmastime too.

Tess had been doing various shifts on and off since Fiona had met her after coming back to work several months earlier. It had worked out well and the two had become close, forming a circle of friends that Fi could never have predicted to possibly exist as it included Reuben but not Jonathan. It was odd how things worked out; she had barely known Reuben before Jonathan had died. Fi stirred her coffee with her legs crossed on the long table in the special collections department and thought about him as the two women chatted. It was nearing the end of the day and many students had shifted their entire studying process to their dorms or actually begun their exams by this point. Tess and Fi were the only ones in the department, and although the door was open, the glass wall showed that no students were milling around in the hallways. There was very little to do but prepare for the time off that she would be taking in several days. His smell seemed to linger in her scarf as she breathed in and the coffee reminded her of waking up beside him. Its aroma would cling to the air in their bedroom until they braved the day.

- So, you leave on the 15th then? Of December? And you're back on the 16th of January?
- Yea I think so. It's a pretty long break. University life is going to be hard to leave if I ever change careers.

She had thought about this before with Jonathan. He was lucky. He worked by what was basically his own schedule. Things occasionally got pretty busy, but he would be able to tackle small amounts of work either late in the evening or early in the morning from home when he would otherwise be pointlessly browsing the internet or endlessly reading. Fi's hours were always nine-to-five-thirty, but the university schedule had so many breaks that she frequently enjoyed long weekends and always had the holidays to do with what she pleased. They sorted out the details, with Fiona promising to stay in touch nearer the time she got back in case plans changed or if Tess needed some more time off. It should work well. Fiona could slip away relatively unnoticed.

Five-thirty quickly arrived and the two cups of coffee had long ago run dry. With just a few days left to work until she would leave, Fiona's mind had switched to vacation-mode somewhat already. With help from Tess, she organized the few texts that needed shelving, tucked chairs beneath desks, and gathered her things. Leaving only the security lights on, the two women left the department and parted ways. Unless Tess came to visit in the next few days, they would likely not see each other until after the break; Merry-Christmases were exchanged, as were hugs and goodbyes. Fiona enjoyed the walk home in the dark; winter had properly enveloped the town and several brave snowflakes were doing their best to hold their ground before disappearing against the concrete or blowing further in the wind. Fiona breathed in the familiar smell of her scarf as it was wrapped comfortably around her neck and halfway up her face while she walked.

Despite fierce protestations from Geoff and Clara, Alex had won the battle over who would take Fi to the airport. She was a little pissed that she was not going to be able to play host with Tom for her best friend over the break, but reservedly understood that it was probably a good idea for Fi to get away for a while even though she had been doing well of late.

- Still can't believe you're leaving me alone with Tom for a whole month, bitch.

She sipped slowly from a glass of wine while Fiona carefully chose clothes and placed them in her little suitcase. It was still a few days before she would be leaving, but it had become a habit for her to organize her things as soon as they came out of the wash every time she took a trip anywhere.

- Yep. You'll be fine. Until Reuben comes over of course, and you just know he'll bring Karen. Maybe you guys could play charades or something. You'd *love* that wouldn't you.

Fi shot Alex her best sarcastic straight face before allowing it to break and letting her smile snap through quickly.

- That honestly sounds awful. Christmas won't be the same without you here babe. Are you going to go and see Jonathan's parents before you head out?
- Yea I'm sure I will. I think it would break Geoff's heart if I just left.

The two continued chatting until it got late enough for Alex to call it a night. She had ceased on the wine a while earlier as she had to drive.

- Alright, I'll see you in a few days then. Tom probably won't come to the airport. He's working a lot now so that he will be able to take some actual time off over the break.
- Yea sounds good. See you in a few.

Just before Alex was about to leave, she turned on the spot as if remembering something extremely important. She placed her hand on her friend's arm.

- Your PhD application, babe. When is it due?
- Not until February. Don't worry, I'm on it; talking to some potential supervisors etc. Jonathan had been on at me for a while so I guess the wheel was already in motion by the time I picked things back up.
- Well he's a smart guy, then. We will definitely have it all sorted for you as soon as you get back. And you can e-mail me stuff while you're away too.
- Yea it's fine. It's not like I'm going to sub-Saharan Africa to some small village without phone service.

Fiona closed the door behind her friend after sharing their second round of goodbyes and turned back to face her apartment. It felt empty for the first time since she'd moved in. The colour that she had tried to introduce seemed washed out and older than it had done through more alert eyes. Alex had unknowingly taken the warmth and colour with her as she left. Jonathan's face smiled back through pictures that lined her walls between blown-out candles and empty coffee mugs. She slid her back down against her door and cried aloud with her head resting on her knees and her arms wrapped around herself. She had moved to Scotland alone. That trip was far more daunting, but she was terrified to be taking the journey back to Portland for Christmas without Jonathan by her side. Her bag remained half-packed in her room while she cried in the hallway by the door. It was making her room uninviting and chaotic as it lay open and incomplete. Everything would be ok if she could just sit in the hallway for a while and not face her life for a moment. Her eyes eventually ran dry and her throat became parched from her quietly erratic breathing. She was hurting. To say that she missed Jonathan diminished how she felt. It was of no consolation that others had gone through the same or worse. She needed him back. Feelings of anger coursed through her momentarily which were aimed towards him for having left her alone. She immediately felt terrible for having scolded him in her mind and stilled herself. *This trip is meant to be the right decision; it'll be good to see Mom.* Kathy would be the surety for Fiona's sanity during the time she spent in Portland. It would be odd to see people she knew but no longer actually *knew*. She worried that her mum would fall into the same category. Her train of thought soon became too much and her mental images soon laid one atop the other in a collage so obtuse that they quickly disappeared into a greyness that momentarily allowed her to forget what had caused the overflow and she could move on.

Fiona eventually straightened her arms behind her and lifted herself to her feet. She went to her bedroom and brushed her suitcase carefully to the ground. It would be strange to fit everything of her own in her own suitcase again. She had not had to suffer such a hardship since meeting Jonathan as every trip they took began with her, in similar fashion to the space in their rooms, using a great deal of the available space in his suitcase as well as her own. She crawled into bed with her clothes on and pulled the covers high around her head so that she could close herself in and try to stop the world around her from turning. She knew, somewhere, that a good night of sleep would make her feel better and change her perspective by the morning, but she would have given anything to spend that night with Jonathan and feel him breathing as she fell asleep. Her arm rested on the mattress beside her as she faced outwards towards the wall. His face had always kept a troubled expression as he slept, and however small it was, she was sure she could diminish whatever hardships he experienced behind his eyes with her touch. Her feet were cold despite the warm socks that she had neglected to remove. She missed pressing her cold toes and feet between Jonathan's legs to warm them up. He would complain jokingly, suggesting that she used him only for things like that. He could not have been more wrong. After rolling fitfully and pushing the image of Jonathan's pale face cradled in the metal fragments of their car from her mind, she eventually drifted off; her feet remained cold throughout the night.

---

24 - Fiona – December 16th

Work had long since passed and Fiona stood at the foot of her bed, staring into her fully-packed suitcase while clutching a hot cup of tea. The tea-bag tag fluttered over the back of her hand while she contemplated her mental checklist so she carefully wound it around the handle of the mug and slowly sipped – it was still too hot but she had plenty of time. Alex would soon arrive and make a judgement about the amount of baggage that Fi would be taking with her for her trip. *I'll put the kettle on again now so there'll be tea for her when she gets here.* Fiona sat on the floor of the kitchen while the kettle heated up. The noise grew loud and consistent as she sipped her tea and waited for her friend. Geoff and Clara's voices sprang into her head as she waited: "You shouldn't wear your jacket inside or you won't feel the benefit when you head out." She laughed audibly as Alex came through the front door that she had left unlocked. They were family and she knew them in many ways better than her own family, but their accents and mannerisms still tickled her often.

- What's so funny? And why are you sat on the floor, weirdo?
- Nothing, just being a kid for a moment. Do you want tea?

Alex gestured with her own mug while looking around for the things that they needed to take to the car.

- I'm good thanks, babe. Let's get your shit together. Also, its bloody freezing outside so you're going to be fucked now that you've worn your coat in here. Nice work.

Fi laughed again and flicked the kettle off. It took both women, who felt like girls by the time the task was done, to lift Fiona's giant suitcase down the stairs of her building and into the back of Alex's car.

The air was biting outside and Fiona felt as though she was ill-equipped for the conditions. The same wind had aggressively brushed her face when she had gone to Spain with Jonathan. They left at five in the morning when the sky was

145

still dark and the cool of the air made the insides of her nostrils tingle as she breathed in.

- Okay. Do we have everything?

Jonathan's voice was calm despite the fact that they were running a little late.

- Yea, we're good.

They had a few hours to drive as they had booked out of a different airport, so Fi had brought her laptop into the front seat so that she could properly DJ for the start of their journey regardless of the early hour of the morning. She was already in her flip-flops and sundress despite the cool, Scottish air descending upon them as they got in the car. After several songs they both knew, Fiona took it upon herself to find something that might surprise Jonathan or make him reasonably uncomfortable and question her taste. She scrolled through her music carefully between selecting safe songs, looking for the *right* one. She passed "Kiss Me" by Sixpence None the Richer, she almost clicked on "Breakfast at Tiffany's" by Deep Blue Something and "Baby" by Justin Bieber before landing on the right choice.

- *Here's, how it goes. You and me, up and down but baby this time...*

Fiona nearly snapped her neck turning her head to face Jonathan so quickly. She could not contain the shock and excitement she felt when he sang to the song with her. She would have, unquestionably, bet the balance of her student loan on the fact that he would either not have known the song or have hated it.

- *We'll, get it right. It's worth the fight. 'Cause love is something you can't shake, when it breaks, all it takes, is some trying.*

Laughing loudly, the two of them burst into the chorus of Enrique's "Escape" and flawlessly made it to the end as they headed towards the airport. Neither had said the words yet, but she knew she loved him. If not for all the things she knew about him, then certainly for all the things she had yet to learn. She put her computer on the floor in front of her chair and curled her legs beneath her on the passenger's seat. She held Jonathan's hand on the gearstick as he drove and felt that it was in the right place for the first time. A small smile rested on his face as he drove through the early morning towards the sunrise.

The trip to the airport with Alex was more subdued. Fi stared out of the window while Alex, characteristically, drove much too quickly. Her hand traded duties of gear changes and bringing her mug carefully to her lips as she drove and talked endlessly. The radio hummed quietly in the background of the conversation but neither of them paid it any attention. It was right that they refrained from singing along to any Enrique or Sixpence None the Richer. It would have seemed as though the memory was being stolen or replaced. *Alex wouldn't sing along anyway, bless her heart but she'd think it was stupid.* Clad in her most comfortable travelling clothes – sweatpants, flats, a tank top and a purple hoodie beneath her winter coat and scarf – Fiona settled into the short drive and prepared herself for the ordeal of air-travel facing her for the next day or so. Her hair was long enough to be tied back now with the assistance of some bobby-pins holding the few stray hairs in place. The tension created by her hairband was slowly giving her a headache as though she had to strain to keep her head forwards and prevent keeling over backwards as a result of the pull from behind.

- I think this year's Christmas day will end up being pretty tame over here...

Alex had started another conversation without realizing that Fi had barely been present in its predecessor. It was comforting to hear the mingling of Alex's voice with the low hum of the radio news presenter.

They pulled around into the airport parking lot "drop-off" zone where Alex quickly and efficiently unloaded the bag that had caused the two of them so many problems at the start of the journey. She promptly hugged her friend and shared a few parting words. Alex was sensible enough to avoid sentimentality, comfortable in the knowledge that a month was not a long time and internet and phone connections made things that much easier still.

- See you soon, babe.
- Yea, have a good Christmas with the guys, eh!

They laughed and quickly parted ways. Alex checked her phone for the time and moved with the efficiency that came undoubtedly from the knowledge that if she stayed too long in the "drop-off" zone, her parking fee would increase dramatically. She quickly pulled away and filtered into the row of cars disappearing around the corner of the parking structure. Fi watched it slide away and caught sight of the sky from far away inside the tower. It was still dark. She began to do the calculations and conversions of the time and ensured it was currently late in the evening in Portland where her mum would be waiting and checking her phone for updates of Fi's travel itinerary. As she walked towards the main terminal to check in, she realized she probably would not get to see much of the sunlight for the next day or so, aside from through the oval plane windows at which time she intended to do nothing but sleep.

She was soon through security. It had been a relatively relaxed process compared to some of her experiences in America. Slipping her flats back on and pulling her small carry-on bag behind her, Fi searched for her gate and a spot in which she could relax for a while. Although it was early, plenty of people filed through the terminal, some with a great sense of haste, others with the curiosity of children — perhaps they had never flown before — and others with the meandering pace of pensioners walking a circuit through the local mall for their daily or weekly exercise. It was a gamble when choosing where to sit, particularly when the task was undertaken alone. Had Jonathan accompanied her, it would not have mattered if the two had sat directly next to a loud or sprawling group as she could nestle beside him and they could really make the most of the real-estate that sharing two adjacent chairs offered. When sitting alone, the bubble one needs to create around him or herself negatively impacts the amount of useable space. Heaven forbid that one's belongings should spread to another chair on a busy day otherwise you become *that girl* or *that guy*. With that in mind, the unfortunate solo-traveller is destined to spend her waiting time in the central eighty to eighty-five percent of their selected chair so as to remain safe from criticism and refrain from intruding into other travellers' space.

Fiona carefully selected a spot near enough to her gate without having to socialize with the other travellers, save being caught in a conversation with a chatty passenger on the same flight who just happened to have the ticket for the seat next to hers. *This is safe here. I'm far enough but close enough I'm sure.* There were a few vacant seats to either side of her. She quickly inserted her earbud headphones without actually queuing any music and evaluated the space around her. Her carry-on bag had quickly become her footrest ahead of her so that she would not have to place her feet on the neighbouring chairs. Most of the other passengers in her vicinity were in pairs. There were groups of students, older couples, businessmen looking tired, and the occasional solo traveller like herself. It was easier for her to pretend that she was not a part of the final group. Jonathan was simply elsewhere in the airport, fetching her something that she needed for the flight. There was a coldness about travelling alone. It permeated her mood and allowed its long fingers to stretch beneath her scarf and breathe the stale terminal air across her skin, rendering it a field of goosebumps in an instant. She wrapped her scarf around her neck more closely and continued to people-watch.

The mouths of those in pairs and groups seemed constantly in motion compared to hers which remained closed and still without any necessary words to share. The couple nearest to her looked happy. They were young; early to mid twenties at the oldest. The girl lay with her feet in her boyfriend's lap and her head rested two seats down on her little backpack. *Apparently they had no regard for the seat rules.* The boy passed one hand up and down his partner's leg while staring off into space. He looked tired, but a different kind of tired to that of the businessmen. The boy had been awake because he wanted to be. He had stayed up with his girlfriend, they had spent time with their friends before going home for the holidays. He was happy. *Are they going back to his parents' or hers this time? Are they nervous? Could be the first time for either of them to cross that line.* The girl adjusted herself without taking her eyes off of her phone. Neither looked concerned or worried.

Further away an old couple sat in relative silence. Unlike the "youths," they sat side by side, only touching by proxy as the fabric of their jackets overlapped in the space between their legs on the seat-bench. Fiona watched them move slowly next to each other for several minutes. *They must be late sixties. He looks a little younger than her. Is that what we would have looked like?* There was something more intimate about the way the two people sat than the way the youths interlaced their limbs across each other not twenty feet away. The years they had, according to Fiona, obviously shared together were much more binding than the others' touch could possibly be. Fiona decided that these people had been married for over forty years. They were similar to Geoff and Clara, only the gentleman didn't look worried or tired; he looked at peace. Fiona decided that this man could neither be Jonathan nor Geoffrey. *Maybe the line's on Jonathan's face would have traced a different path to Geoff's; maybe in his sixties he would have had that kind of peace.* Perhaps the gentleman was happy at the prospect of a full day on the plane when he could sit and watch movies or sleep without anyone telling him he needed to do other things. *I should really stretch a little bit before I get on the plane, it's a crazy long time to just be sat still otherwise.* As the older woman stood up to leave and run a quick errand, the old man's face clicked into gear and into motion as he gestured to help her stand. He mouthed words that Fiona was sure were an offering of help or assistance. When the lady declined and walked away, their hands quickly brushed by one another and Fi could almost feel the connection and electricity they still felt from across the room. Neither had yet lost the other one.

   Breathing out in what she thought may have been frustration mixed with a little boredom, Fi switched her gaze towards the few other travellers who were making their way across the world at Christmastime without a travel companion; the group into which she reluctantly fell. There were five or six such people within eyeshot. All had their headphones in except for one. He looked about thirty. He was heavyset, bearded, and intensely concentrated on his book. The others in the *group* shared the same vacant expression that Fiona had perfected over her twenty-seven years. Out of self-pity, Fiona wondered who from this group had lost what she had lost. Who else was going home following the death of their husband or wife for Christmas? She imagined a tragedy for each of these people and projected her own onto them. Their expressions remained the same throughout her narratives. The most shocking of circumstances had led to the deaths of each of these traveller's wives and husbands or girlfriends and boyfriends. This exercise solidified Fiona's membership into such a group. She at once felt the chasm opening between herself and the two couples on her right at each end of their respective relationships. Her bond with the *solos* was becoming stronger as she added more and more detail to the impossibly terrible circumstances under which each of their lives had been derailed in the past year. They, too, would have to put on their strongest faces and stand up straight as they returned home to answer questions and say "I'm fine" on repeat until they almost believed it to be true or until they ran out of breath and fell backwards into the spaces their minds had reserved for escape.

It took an airport-wide announcement to break her from her train of thought and snap her back to the reality of the situation. When she looked back across the room at the expressions of those whose lives she had destroyed, she became aware of the lack of impact she had exerted upon them. They continued with their journeys and with their waiting. Their lives continued to tick forward as did everything else; as did hers. Fiona removed her earbuds and contemplated a short walk through the terminal. She had plenty of time and would need to use the bathroom before boarding. Rounding the corner of her internal pity-session, she instead began to feel pity towards others. *Who is our windbreaker friend spending the holidays with?* She knew Alex and Tess thought the guy was weird. He absolutely was, but there was no need for him to be having an unpleasant experience over the break when everyone else spent their time with family and loved ones. She hadn't understood what he'd meant before regarding his previous partner. She was not even sure if he had been with a man or a woman, if he was married or not, or if there was any relationship whatsoever to which he was referring. *He seems like a Toby.* It had been too long since their first interaction for Fiona to appropriately ask his name. He knew hers, and she had missed the opportunity to ask it back on that occasion. Since then they had spoken a number of times in the library and the window of opportunity had disappeared entirely. All the same, she decided he would be Toby.

"The airport is currently in a heightened state of security. It is the responsibility of all passengers and airport staff to ensure the continued safety of..." Fiona walked through the airport with her carry-on trailing behind her and intermittently heard several of the announcements during the lulls in her music. Having heard the conversations of the nearby parties in real time, she had been compelled to retreat back into her playlist until her journey was over. *Toby is with his family this Christmas. Toby is not alone this Christmas. Toby will return to a welcoming home and a family that loves him.* She laughed quietly to herself as she could not imagine him without his windbreaker. As he sat at the table for a Christmas dinner, surrounded by faceless bodies in Fiona's imagination, his grey and blue windbreaker still shuffled quietly amongst the frivolity of the occasion. *Did all his friends and family wear the same ones?* He cracked a half smile and shed some of the weight that he seemed to always carry. Fiona hoped it was not pity she felt towards him but was almost sure that it was. Her thoughts had brought her all the way back to her gate and she quickly found the seat she had vacated. Jonathan had promised that they would never travel alone. She understood why.

---

25 - Jonathan – December 10th

Jon slammed the door hard and stormed up the driveway to his parents' house. He ignored the doorbell and instead banged hard repeatedly on the black, wooden door to the house in which he'd grown up. Inside he heard Clara's voice calling for Geoff in something sounding distinctly like concern. He stepped back to view the upstairs window and saw the curtains twitch a little before settling; the sound of slow, heavy footsteps descending the stairs was audible through the door. Geoff opened it and bore a bewildered expression. Jon took no notice whatsoever of his father's face, brushed passed him with his boots on, and headed straight for the kitchen at the end of the hall. His mother, who had been observing from the top of the staircase immediately sprang to life.

- Jon, darling come on. You know how mucky and wet it is outside right now. This is why we have to get the bloody carpet re-done so often!

She was angry but was ill-practiced at expressing it. She also evidently knew that Jon was angry about something and would not have a voice loud enough to compete with his.

- What's going on Jon? Why all the bloody banging and noise?

Jon turned to face his father and ignored the concern and compassion that clearly comprised the lines on his aging face.

- You couldn't just fucking LEAVE IT ALONE could you!
- What are you talking about?
- You had to go over there and fucking play "Dad" again didn't you?
- Jon, calm it down mate.

If Geoff understood what Jon was upset about, he didn't show it. This had the effect of worsening Jon's mood and further accelerating his temper.

- Look, just sit down mate and let's have it out. I've clearly done something to piss you off pretty hard.

Geoff had decided some days earlier that he understood why his son had been let go from the university. He was sure it was to do with Jon's overnight stay at the police station somehow getting back to those in charge. After many discussions with his wife, he had evidently taken it upon himself to try to remedy the situation and try to get Jon his position back at the university. After making a trip over there and talking to some people who he was relatively sure were closely connected to Jon's work, he had done his best to explain the situation with Fiona and how Jon had been struggling to cope with things of late. He had assured these people that Jon was doing much better, that he had rounded a corner in recent weeks, and that he was more than capable of continuing his role as he had always proven himself to be trustworthy and reliable.

Jon knew of all such details through a confused and bewildered sounding email he had opened the day before on his phone – he had yet to replace his laptop since sweeping it to the ground in his emotional fit some weeks earlier. Jon's emotional outburst abated briefly and in its intermission he explained the email to his father.

- I don't get what you're so upset about… I was just trying to help you out mate.
- Well DON'T Okay?
- Why?
- Because that wasn't even why I was fucking fired, Okay?

Jon's words trailed off as he finished his sentence and he slumped himself into one of the black leather chairs surrounding the dining room table.

- Happy?
- What are you talking about?

Jon cracked his knuckles getting about five out of eight to chime off. He was embarrassed and angry.

- Why did they let you go mate?
- It's been month's since I've submitted anything. I stopped working a few weeks after Fiona died. I haven't been contributing to the university since then.

Geoff pulled out a chair at the table, leaving a few spaces between he and his son. Jon was looking blankly at the table in front of him and rubbing his thumbs against his index and middle fingers as he waited for whatever would happen next. He could hear his mother shuffling around upstairs, obviously trying to "stay out of the way" but also doing her best to eavesdrop on the whole conversation.

- I didn't know that. I was trying to help you.
- Well you shouldn't have, should you?

Jon's voice was beginning to rise again. His tone had passed swiftly through the intermittent lull and was gearing back up towards aggression. Geoff sensed it quickly and stood up to get a drink from the kitchen.

As Jon turned to his father without getting up from his own seat, he opened his mouth to continue his angry monologue but Geoff beat him to it.

- You know what Jon. I don't have to have you come into my house and raise your voice at me for the mistakes you've made. You can't be honest with yourself about how hard things are for you. You lie to your family, whether it's by omission or not, about what you're doing, and then lash out at the first person that tries to help you.

Jon opened his mouth again to interject but was again shut down as it was clearly Geoff's turn. He had not seen or heard his father become so impassioned in a long time.

- None of us mate, none of us have any idea what you're going through. We GET that you don't want to share everything and that you have kept whatever healing process you have to yourself, but don't you dare start treating the people around you like crap because we don't have the fucking x-ray vision to see what the hell is going on between your god damn ears.

Jon heard, saw, and felt the words leave his father's mouth. The intensity was tangible and he understood why Clara was hiding out upstairs. He then quickly forgot about Fiona. He forgot that she was singing at home; waiting for him. She was still there in his mind, of course. He forgot himself in the process and abruptly stood from his chair and made for the door. Something gave way in the space between his now burning ears. Either a snap or a melting away of a vital sinew or tendon that had been clinging to life for what seemed like eons. He had to get out. Whatever was going on in his mind had turned to cotton-wool. His thoughts seemed drunk and circled one another inside his head without order or reason. The heat stretched down his back and up his arms as it had done for months, and he did his best to make a wordless escape from the claustrophobia of the kitchen and from this home that stifled and suffocated everything. Geoff, however, was not ready to let his son out of his sight just yet. He had reached the point where the silent process had officially failed and he needed to have it out. The clash was imminent but neither was aware until the deed had been done.

Jon reacted swiftly and instinctively when his father grabbed his arm to stop him from leaving. He turned and swung hard, sending the old man staggering backwards for a few steps before falling onto his back. Jon had turned away before seeing his father reach the ground. He heard the sound of his mother scampering quickly down the stairs and calling after him but the sound seemed far away with an echo in his ears. Without turning to answer, he got back into his car and sped out of the driveway.

Geoff sat on the floor in a sense of disbelief over what had just happened. His hands shook by his sides as his wife entered the room in what seemed like slow-motion. His field of vision seemed eclipsed by a border of haze and he wondered if this was due to the adrenaline of the argument or from the hit he had taken to his right temple less than a minute earlier. He stared down the empty hallway towards the open front door and his eyes remained wide for quite some time. When he finally brought his arm up to wipe his forehead it came back red, but he felt no pain. *That's definitely the adrenaline, it's going to hurt an awful lot later.* His legs lay splayed open in front of him in what looked like a lazy butterfly-stretch. Clara was busying herself with wetting a small towel for his forehead. He gently stroked her leg when she sat beside him on the kitchen floor and tended to his cut. She was crying about the situation, evidently concerned over what would happen next. Neither she nor Geoff had expected Jon's reaction, regardless of the situation. Geoff failed to notice the small beads of sweat forming on his forehead or the tears that also rolled down his own face. He spoke sternly; resolute.

-   It's okay love. I'll sort it out. It's okay.

His hand opened and closed from a palm to an unclenched fist repeatedly. It reassured Clara that things would be somehow smoothed over. It was a gesture that Geoffrey and his father had shared and one that she and Fiona had seen Jonathan emulate during times of trouble; it was an approach she wished he'd taken this time. The front door had swung all the way open revealing the empty space on the drive where Jonathan had pulled away in a haste.

158

- I hope he doesn't drive too bloody fast wherever he's going.

The two stayed on the kitchen floor for a long time. It was Geoff who eventually decided to move things on and get up. He did so slowly, using the kitchen counter to help him stand. He wiped the remainder of the blood from the side of his face on the towel and hung it over his shoulder. He filled the kettle at the sink before heading to the front door to close it and keep the cool air out, then returned to help his wife back up.

She would be alright. Geoffrey Eliot's calmness was a resounding force over the now clearing situation. Almost visible in the old couple's eyes, the dust settled in the kitchen and the kettle clicked off, ready and willing to return the room to a state of comparative normalcy. Geoff had seen only a moment too late some part of the lights going out inside Jonathan's head; a visual manifestation of the hole that had been dug deep within him by Fiona's death. The hole was worsened and decayed further by Jon's response to it all. Thanks to a lifetime of experience and resilience, Geoff's hands no longer shook as he poured from the kettle. A small drop of blood landed a few inches from one of the cups he filled so he tilted his head back until the task was complete before wiping himself up again and cleaning his new mess on the counter.

- I haven't seen him like that before. I thought he was getting better. It was all just crap though, eh.
- We should have probably seen it sooner, right?

Clara and Geoff stood quietly in the kitchen with mugs of tea steaming behind them on the counter. Their tired faces bore the same expressions they had worn a decade earlier after school fights or suspensions, or when David decided he would stop trying at anything and smoke cigarettes he would later realize made him run slower and look like a twat. Geoff's face remained stoic and firm as older men's faces do. The lines that Jonathan would one day inherit were etched across his skin, outlining the journey that had unpredictably brought him to the present. His eyes had ceased to be so wide and the sweat on his forehead had slowed to a mere trickle, allowing only the most persistent of beads to sneak through. Akin to his son's recent behaviour, he reached into the kitchen drawer for some painkillers for his head and washed them down with a mouthful of tea.

---

26 - Jonathan – December 25th

It had taken Jon a long time to return to himself. To say that he'd made it all the way back would have been a lie. Waking up on Christmas morning alone was something he was not used to. He realized the significance of the day after turning the radio on in the kitchen because he was tired of hearing the same song from Fiona through the hallways. His memories of her had begun to meld into a rerun cycle that was becoming less and less adept at mimicking reality. Reuben had called to abuse him several times since hearing about his outburst from his parents and had clearly given up in favour of spending the holidays with his new girlfriend being blissfully happy, sickly, and affectionate all over the place and all over every poor observer's field of view. It was something people like Jon just could not unsee after the fact. He was sure he had once been the one causing the emotional chagrin as passers-by witnessed his happiness with Fiona, although it felt like a much longer period of time had actually passed since Fiona's death.

Jon had returned to wearing glasses around the house. Perhaps Fiona had once mentioned that he looked good wearing them or that they suited him in some way. He could no longer remember. He rubbed the bridge of his nose with thumb and forefinger and traipsed about his house making a slapdash breakfast with the radio humming from his phone. Rather than adding a sense of wisdom to his appearance as he believed glasses might, they had the effect of roughening his appearance and adding to the "homeless" vibe he emanated in his white t-shirt and boxers. If he was a scientist or if he had written a successful screenplay, his look may have been acceptable; he, of course, had done neither. Every few minutes the music or conversation dimmed as his phone alerted him that he was avoiding his life. There were texts and calls waiting from numerous people. He felt a part of something larger, though, as it was Christmas morning. There would always be that tsunami of text messages and alerts from friends not seen for years or from family paying their dues. *Will I get any texts or messages addressed to both of us? Does anyone not know about it all? Probably someone somewhere.* This wave would sweep across his screen early in the morning and wane by the evening as the last stragglers would keep up with the convention. Jon wouldn't be alone in receiving this barrage of communication on Christmas. He could happily ignore it all without being the only one to do so as he sat back in his office chair and sipped a black coffee with his usual crushed mess floating from top to bottom.

A loud, repetitive banging on the front door shook Jon from the relative trance of his coffee-concoction. Contrary to what he had thought, Roob had not given up. *Persistent little bastard he's become.*

- Don't be a twat. It's Christmas. Open the fucking door mate.

Jon looked at his watch expressionlessly as he walked to the door. His mind was focused on his coffee as he wondered what it's general effect would be. He had crushed his typical painkillers into its midst. Along with making the pain in his back tolerable, they would have the effect of making him sleepy based on the excessive amount he took each time. The coffee was meant to work towards waking him, but it rarely did. He pushed out his bottom lip as he neared the door and left his coffee as something that he would never really understand; such a list had been growing considerably of late.

- Reuben!

Jon opened the door with a fake, sarcastic smile and a condescending tone of frivolity. Roob pushed him backwards hard and the coffee in Jon's mug made waves over the rim and left hot, bruise-coloured splotches on the kitchen floor.

- Your breath smells about as bad as you do mate. Get your shit together, you're coming out today.
- Well it's lovely to see you, too Roob. Merry fucking Christmas.

Roob looked around the kitchen, somewhat surprised to see that the place was relatively clean and tidy. Fiona's coffee pot remained untouched as it had done since she had last used it some months ago.

- Karen's made food. She wants to see you-

Jon cut him off before he could properly continue. He held his hand up as something of a silent halt.

- No she doesn't mate, don't be a dick.
- What are you talking about?
- She doesn't even know me. Why would she want me there? You guys go and have your lovely happy little Christmas.

The awkward posture and stance that Roob had perfected over the years was absent on this occasion as Jon regarded him from

162

across the room. *This girl is changing him a fair amount; could be good, though, I guess.* He looked annoyed. His face explained to Jon clearly the sentiment of "well I've tried my fucking best, now I'm leaving you here to be depressed by yourself." What he voiced was much nicer.

- Sorry mate. Started out wrong today I guess. But *I* would really like it if you came and joined us, and I'm not going to stand here and talk about it anymore. So either get your things together or don't, but I'm heading back to Karen now.
- See you later then Reuben.

Jon's voice had become more solemn in the few minutes the two men had been in the same room. It was a change that Roob took quick notice of and chose to leave on that note. He had done more than most would have. He gave Jon a pat on the shoulder has he left and almost felt the ridges of Jon's scar as his fingers brushed away.

- Now you can go pretend to be fucking happy for yourself instead of standing in my shadow for three fucking years eh.

Jon's expression remained stoic and his heartbeat remained steady as he delivered the final comment of the day and quietly sipped from the rest of his drink. Roob did not bite. He paused briefly in the doorway before shaking his head and closing the door on it all.

Grey-white light poured in through the kitchen window over Jonathan Eliot as he stood alone. His Christmas morning was going well. He reeled through the various retorts he was sure that Reuben would have come back with to his argument. It bothered him intensely that he hadn't risen to his comments and given him the opportunity to battle it out. It was only as he stood alone that his heart began to race again and the frustration re-emerged as he heard Fiona starting up

163

with the same songs down the hall. Her padded footsteps added the familiar percussion to the tune he knew too well. *Probably should have fucking gone with Roob...* After downing the sludge remaining in his mug, he put on some jeans and a sweater, tied his boots and headed out for a walk. The air bit at his face as he did so. His beard, growing longer than he had realized, offered protection for his chin and left his cheekbones to brave the cold for themselves as he trudged onwards without direction. They seemed to protrude further than they once had. *Perhaps I've lost more weight under this beard. I'll just walk for a bit, get some fresh air then head home. I should ring mum and dad, too.* The list of notifications on his phone suggested he should call his family. Despite his most recent interaction with them ending in the blow that sent his father to the ground, they still wanted to see him. It was something he had to do, regardless of the situation.

The previous Christmas had been perfect. He realized the walk was the same. His hand felt warm from hers as they had walked with fingers interlaced; this year was colder of course.

- Did your mum get you crazy amounts of presents again darling?
- I don't think so. She might be upset that I didn't go home this year.

Fiona's voice was full of happiness. Her step skipped a little with a bob as each foot raised that she didn't notice. She sprang on noiselessly down the road like a child.

- Well, I promise we'll go see your mum next year for Christmas. I'll just have to work on my mum and dad so that they don't lose their shit.

Fiona rested her head on Jon's arm as they walked together for a little while. It was easy. Jon wore a sincere smile as the two cut down a small lane between overhanging plants and various bushes that were brave enough to stick around for the winter months.

- Or we could go somewhere with actual snow next year?
- *Actual* snow?
- Yea! Like more than Scotland!

There was a playfulness in her voice that showed Jonathan it did not matter. They could go anywhere and it would be fine. Her finger's poked through the vintage-style gloves so she could feel Jon's skin against hers from her mid-knuckles and up; she folded the mitten-caps back every few minutes as the Velcro patch on each of the backs of her hands let loose it's grip and let them fall.

It had been so long since Jon had planned anything. On his walk with Fiona just one year earlier they had planned to be in Portland by now with Kathy for the break; or somewhere with snow, or literally anywhere. As he walked it became clearer that he wasn't heading anywhere. He slowed his stride and looked around as he walked, noticing that there were very few other pedestrians out on the street as he was. Those who shared his Christmas-day pastime walked in pairs as he had done the year before. It was different now. He nodded politely at the passers-by who came close enough to need it and occasionally grunted a stifled expression of what was most likely "Merry Christmas." People smiled back, but as they did, he read what he was sure was pity and confusion permeating their faces. "Why is he walking alone? He must be on his way to meet someone?" *They're all speculating.* Jon allowed the speculation to continue as he abruptly turned back on the lane down which he had been slowly walking for several minutes. He headed back to his house without any idea of what he planned to do once he arrived there. *Last year I was planning a Christmas that was literally a year away, now I don't even know what I'm doing with the next days or hours of my life.* The thought of going home was unappealing at best. Walking was getting him nowhere. Seeing his family was going to be an extremely tense and unpleasant experience. Missing Fiona was something that he had become used to as it hurt him every moment of every day. What he missed as he walked home was the company and safety of doing *nothing* with her. Walking home aimlessly was not aimless when he shared the mindset with Fiona. Her presence gave him a purpose he could not explain, even to himself. She needed no looking after, she never had. All the same, his brain had filled itself with the actions of two for the last three years. The empty space in which his thoughts now bounced around caused things to misfire. The jump from one thing to the next was often too big for him to comprehend; as a result, he remained rooted in place, unable to figure out what was required of him.

Saving him from the black spaces in his blotchy and incomplete mind, his parents called him before he arrived back at his house. Against his better judgement, he answered the call and agreed to spend the afternoon in what was sure to be a strange state of discomfort. They loved him. He was not sure if he still loved them. He had to, really. The idea of it was just something that had left him of late. Loving anything didn't seem bad, it just hadn't crossed his mind. If it had, the jump from one side to the other of any one of the empty spaces in the cosmos of his brain had been too much of an endeavour and the thought had fallen flat and ultimately vanished.

Her time away from Scotland had strangely flown by in a haze of moments that would soon be lost and forgotten among the plethora of Christmas moments from childhood, adolescence, and Jonathan. In whatever way they were to be remembered, they would always be *without* Jonathan. His absence would serve as a marker in her long term memory in years to come when the small moments she recalled would challenge her brain over what point in her life was being recalled. He was not there, that's how she would know when it was. She wondered slowly how others organized their memories in such a way. *Haircuts? Clothes? Music, probably, for a lot of people.* It had been easy for her to remember the "when" of most instances in her life, however small, as she had moved around a great deal more than most people she knew. The apartment she had come home to in Scotland was a quick reminder of that fact. Her dreams and daydreams had yet to feature it as "the place she lived" and she still calculated distances to and from things in relation to the house she had shared with Jonathan as though she was still writing the previous year in the margins of her pages when the calendar neared February at school. *He said I'd see mum this year for Christmas; not quite what I had in mind.* She wondered how many good things she had forgotten; how many bad things had been selectively misplaced in her memory. Even the best of memories were eventually weeded down a highlight reel that became more sepia-toned and replayed in her mind over time.

Going back to work would be a welcome return to the 'new' routine. Fi had chatted with Tess several times about the trivialities of work and the various things that needed to be done. She was looking to start a full time job with the library in some capacity or another during the summer. *It could happen;*

unlikely, though. The library had been open for almost a week after the Christmas break at the university by the time Fiona came back to work, and Tess was waiting for her by the glass door in the morning of her first day back.

- Hey, darling how are you doing? Merry Christmas, happy new year and all that!
- Good thanks Fi, how was your break?

The two chatted as they unlocked and prepped the department for the day together. The lights buzzed on and gradually reached their full potential as Fi and Tess put down their bags and jackets. They knew there would be very little actual shelving to do, but Fi had plenty of emails that needed responding to about orders for new material and auctions for older pieces the university had been trying to acquire. Fi thought about Toby. *I really need to learn his actual name at this point.* She hoped his break had been good. She wondered who he had gone home to, if he had at all, and if he would have flown alone as she did. Before she could think for too long about it, Tess had jumped headfirst into her own Christmas break play-by-play and Fiona dutifully followed along. She asked about Reuben and Karen, they were still doing really well and had spent Christmas in each other's company. Unable to contribute with interesting tales of her own, Fiona played the listener. *Tess will have to go soon and I can actually get some of my work done.* She laughed a little to herself that the department had been open for an hour and there had not been a single visitor and Tess had not ceased her Christmas narrative.

When she eventually left, Fiona sat dutifully at her computer and worked through the orders. An original print of Stephen Dunn's poem "The Vanishings" was on order. It was a much newer piece of work than was usually kept in the special collections department so it must have been a direct student order. She knew the poem well. "One day it will vanish, how it felt when you were overwhelmed." She missed feeling overwhelmed like that. "One day one thing and then a dear other." She moved on quickly in her mind and filtered through the remaining emails. Surprisingly, it took her long past when she would usually have taken her lunch. She resolved instead to just eat what she'd brought at her desk with her feet up in the empty special collections department. It was late in the afternoon by the time the first few students filtered in. While Fi didn't know their names by heart, they were regulars. They sat in *their corner* and worked quietly amongst themselves without need of help or assistance from Fi. She nodded as the group of girls filed in and resumed their practice for the new year. *What are the things that "wouldn't vanish fast enough?"* Dunn's work was still in her mind despite having stared at a long list of other titles since working through the order. It was good work and it did its job well.

Carrying a few smaller texts and one larger periodical, Fiona sidled into the unseen space between bookshelves to text Alex. She had been left out of the "airport pickup" as Geoff and Clara could not be dissuaded on this occasion. "No" had not been an acceptable answer. Fi had been looking forward to seeing and hearing from Alex for weeks. "Bitch why aren't you visiting me yet! ;)" Alex replied fast but not with the reply that Fi had hoped for. "Sorry babe! Can't wait to see you, got some serious stuff going on at the moment. With Tom today, I'll ring you later!" Fiona slid her phone back into the pocket of her jeans and shelved the materials she had brought with her. They were the most frequently shelved and re-shelved pieces as she usually made a habit of picking them up early in the day to have an excuse to get up and text. They were works she was sure nobody would need, and in the time she had worked in the department, she had been right. Texting was the devil. She thought back to when she was single before Jonathan. The texting life was difficult to navigate and she was on the cusp of being old enough to actually use her phone as a phone. Everyone now seemed to use their phone exclusively to text in some way or another. Jonathan had been an anomaly as he was neither a texter nor a caller. There were no smilies or sad faces in Alex's text, but she had said she would call later in the evening, so there was that to look forward to. *I hope she's alright. There's very little that could possibly cause problems between her and Tom. I could really do with a drink with her later. I'll get wine on the way home.*

The unmistakeable shuffle of the windbreaker removed Fiona from thoughts of phone conversations with Jonathan in her mind. She had lost track of time as the afternoon had passed. His voice had been so calming and peaceful regardless of his mood. When he spoke she could feel his hand brush against hers with skin that was rough enough to make her tingle. Her eyes had glazed as she thought about his smell and how he stood near to her. His chest, at her eye height, would heave gently up and down with his breath. They were in line for something. She looked up and checked his gaze. He was focused on the front of the line in the near distance as they shuffled forwards. Fi made minute steps backwards and clung to the space around him as they moved. It was warm, Jonathan was undoubtedly sweaty as he usually was. Her fingertips touched his chest. Before they even made contact, the heat radiated from him towards her; he was damp to the touch. Responding to her touch he looked down and laughed apologetically for being sweaty. Fiona didn't mind in the slightest. She kissed his chest through his shirt and backed up slightly to give him some room in the hope that it would help to cool him down. Not letting her leave, Jonathan placed a hand gently on the back of her neck beneath her hair as she turned forward to face the front of the line. Hearing the sound of the windbreaker in the library snapped the invisible hand away from her skin and brought her careening back to reality at an unwelcome pace.

The book she had been holding slipped from her fingers and fell into a crumpled heap at her feet between the high walls of the bookshelves.

His voice, on this occasion, was unmistakably clear.

- You didn't tell me you were leaving.

Despite his clarity, she responded by default from the ground as she attempted to scoop up the injured book she had neglected.

- I'm sorry?

Had *Toby* known what he was doing more clearly, his witty retort may have sounded something like "you will be" or "not yet." All he could muster was a single syllable response as he lurched forwards and grabbed Fiona's hair, forcing her face forwards and her chin upwards as he pulled and pushed erratically. Happening as quickly as the car leaving the road had done less than a year earlier, Fiona was whipped along with the situation, unable to comprehend what was going on at any more depth than the pain she felt in the back of her head and neck from her hair doing its best to cling to life. Only moments earlier had Jonathan's hand caressed the spot. This hand was soft and sickly. It had a coldness that one might mistake for porcelain or alabaster had it not moved so deftly. It was already becoming part of her history.

---

28 - Jonathan – January 8th

New year's resolutions had yet to cross Jon's mind as he walked across the university campus. He glanced over to the entrance of the library as he passed, and like a song laced with indeterminate memory triggers, he realized how he felt at the sight of it. The first few bars of the song were pleasant before the memories became too heavy and the tones became sour and overused. Such was the effect of his view. A young woman, who he was sure was called Tess, walked briskly with a shoulder bag — it looked Southeast Asian, some hippie style — slung across her towards the door and disappeared into the darkness of the building. *She's Karen's friend, I think.* He remembered seeing her at some outing or another several months earlier. He had glazed over at the conversation as he heard where she worked. *She must be Fiona's replacement.* It was a twisted choreography to replace people in such a way, but had he seen it from outside it would not have taken even an instant of his time in thought. He walked onwards with the scene of Fiona's department fresh in his mind. There she would not be replaced.

- Hey kid.

He had finished his work early some months before the crash and visited Fiona at work at the end of the day. She'd already locked up but she unlatched the door and let him in while she cleaned up, ensuring that the door locked behind him. He sidled in awkwardly, well aware that he was not supposed to be there and also fractionally embarrassed at being out of his element in a scene he did not know well. There was something that had felt untoward or risqué about being in the department alone "after hours" with students milling back and forth on the opposite side of the glass some twenty feet away from them.

- Hey darling, how are you?

She stood up on tiptoes and kissed him while still holding a collection of books that had to be shelved before she could leave. Instinctively, Jon rested his hands on her hips and took on her weight as she leaned forward to kiss him.

It was not the first time they had been alone where Fi worked, but they apparently both picked up on the element of danger offered by the glass walls, the latched door, and the spot they knew too well from which Fiona frequently texted her friends. It was concealed but open; private but voyeuristic. Jon traced his hands up Fiona's back as she put down her work and they moved quickly in tandem towards the space between the high shelves. It must have been summer as they had worn few clothes to begin with. Jon's breath was quiet, long, and drawn out. Fiona bit her lip between kisses and her breath quickened. Jon's rough and searching palms had found their way beneath her sundress. Her flats stayed on with her toes pointed inwards at the floor as she rested her weight back onto the heavy books lining the lower shelves. Jon's face remained stoic and concentrated as he looked after his wife. His eyes passed over their surroundings, adjusting to the light that poured in from the canyon between the bookshelves, to the comparative darkness of the alleyway in which they found themselves. He briefly regarded the beige and green standard university tiled-carpet, wondering how comfortable this would soon be for Fiona's back and bare arse. One arm at a time, he slid swiftly from the confines of his jacket and let it fall to the ground behind him, carefully replacing his arms against Fiona's skin one after the other.

Fiona rested her weight backwards, half-seated against the shelves. Her palms faced down on the shelf she chose as she threw her head back, letting her hair drape over the adjacent books while Jon explored the topography of her neck and chest, bristling his beard gently over the bare skin her sundress displayed. Her breath quickened further as his face searched her skin and she lost where she was. *There are noises coming from outside the room. Students are wondering at the lights being on while the door is locked.* Jon's breath took its turn to quicken as Fi placed her hands on either side of his neck as she sat before him while he stooped over her. She ran her fingers down the unblemished and un-scarred skin of his back, reaching the top of his jeans, sliding beneath the fabric of his loose-fitting cotton shirt and working back up. She had lifted her feet now and wrapped them around the backs of Jon's calves, leaving her flats lying empty on the ground. Gently pulling her hair back, Jon returned to kiss Fiona's neck before taking on her weight with one arm and standing tall, carrying her between the shelves, further into the increasingly darkened and hidden vestibule they shared.

---

29 - Fiona – January 17th 5:36pm

It was hurting her. She didn't understand. None of it was clear in her mind as she was being forced into the space between the shelves, deeper into to the darkness by a stranger. Her hands and wrists ached and grazed as *Toby* forced her forwards onto the green and beige striped carpet; he was remarkably strong given his size compared to hers. She was immediately angry at herself for having been so easy to come about and intimidate. Her heart raced in her chest and pounded hard, dulling the surrounding silence. The room quickly seemed full of water as the blood pulsing through her body rushed past her ears and she drowned. For a moment, her face rested against the rough fibers of the carpet in the darkness. Her hands lay either side of her head as she rested on her stomach. In the quiet intermission period of the surreal nightmare, no hands or alien skin touched hers or tried to move her. *Perhaps it was over. He had left. He had done all he intended to do.*

- FUCK!

Fiona screamed aloud and cursed as a firm palm and flexing, white-knuckled fingers forced her face hard into the ground. The light entering the crevasse between the bookshelves was blotted out by Toby's ever-shifting shadow looming over her and forcing her downwards. The pale face she had come to know was now silhouetted in the periphery of her view as she struggled to look upwards at her attacker. Uttering his name was a fruitless endeavour and screaming for him to stop was increasingly difficult as his weight upon her was pressing the life out of her. With each exhalation or frantically uttered syllable, she sank further into the ground and envisioned becoming completely flat beneath Toby's weight and grasp. Momentary relief was found as Toby released his pressure on her back, but Fiona could merely gasp like a free-diver finally surfacing before being rolled on to her back to be constricted once more by Toby's unusually strong grip. His hands must have been warm by now, but their presence felt cold and searching near her. At each moment when he lifted his palms and fingers from the surface of her skin, it seemed to peel off as though it had been frozen or stuck to metal in the cold. Fi flinched at every close encounter his fingers made and audibly moaned and winced at their eventual and inevitable contact.

Facing him, then, was far worse. His face showed anxiety and more years than he had lived of trouble. He was not calculated in his actions; no part of his behaviour resembled the actions of a villain or psychopath. Toby was a child. He cried like a child. He struggled to free himself from his windbreaker with one hand pressed hard on Fiona's throat

175

as she clawed away at his wrist and struggled to breathe. Removing his brown leather belt and opening the button to his faded and stained jeans was done with a slapdash dexterity that screamed *nerves and fear*. Toby was a child; he was sad. He would be the little boy who would take what did not belong to him, and he would know how wrong it was. He would cry long after. Fiona could only focus on his face from behind a thin water-veil glassing her eyes as they too did their best to cry out for her salvation. It was a salvation she knew would not come for her. As if understanding the futility of her situation, and the tragedy of Toby's, the tension in Fiona's grip around Toby's wrist and the strength in her legs to kick away at his advances lessened and weakened. The vacant stare and glaze in her eyes returned as she felt her clothes being removed from her. It was all far away, though. She had left herself lying on the carpet. She watched as a young man cried. He struggled and fought against her limp frame as he went about his work. The water that had filled the room as her blood had coursed through her only minutes earlier now served to drown her in a different way. She lay calmly and sadly, writhing only gently as though it were the right thing to do in her lifeless state, as the water in her mind seemed to wash around her and silenced the small grunts and sounds escaping Toby's terrified face.

The waves moved her body as he did. It was slow; as if muted in the depth and distance of her situation. Her hands had fallen exhausted and flat by her sides, only occasionally reaching up in sharp jerks at moments of pain which were otherwise concealed by her distance from herself. The hands that searched the now frozen topography of her skin beneath her clothes, worked with a hasty confusion and shaking fright. They shared contact with Fiona's skin now, not only with each other, as Toby neared the end of his work. Fiona whispered, out of breath and hurting from far away.

- I'm sorry Toby. *I'm sorry Toby.*

If he heard what she had uttered, he didn't show it. Fiona rolled her head backwards on the ground. Amidst the strands of her own hair obscuring her view, she looked behind her from the ground towards the darkness of the space between the shelves. For a moment, it went on forever. As her eyes adjusted, the last strands of light making their way beyond her torture illuminated his outline against the gloom. With the calmness of the water surrounding her, her eyes filled the spaces of the body she saw. Jonathan faced her calmly from between the shelves and fixed his gaze upon her.

- I love you.

She reached her arms slowly upwards behind her head towards her husband as she quietly mouthed her three-word retreat from reality.

---

30 - Jonathan – January 8th

Still lost in his memories, Jon caressed his wife's neck between the shelves as he carried her deeper into the darkness. Her legs, wrapped around his own, hoisted upwards until her weight sat around his waist. Jon held her safely in his arms, confident in his knowledge that he would never drop her. With her legs apart, straddling his body, her sundress had become raised up and bunched above her hips. Her grey and purple underwear concealed the rest of her well as it moved and shifted across her cunt as she pressed herself harder against his waist. His hands were warm as they searched her back, the veins in his forearms pulsed and pressed hard against her back as he supported her weight. There was something different about each of their encounters when they made love, with the familiarity and trust in each other that ensured it was just fine when it turned from love-making to fucking.

Jon was carefully forward with his handling, leaving imprints of his own skin and his wife's against the surfaces that acted as their walls from the outside world. Books were knocked and shifted in place on their shelves, sliding out of place and lending a *broken-windows* vibe of disarray to the den that the two created. Fiona reached her arms out in support on several of the larger volumes at her height while she rode in Jonathan's arms and leaned back while he kissed her chest. Her grasp pulled countless texts and volumes from their homes, sending them into a crumpled mess on the ground between Jonathan's feet. The mess had purpose. It was *meant* to be that way. They both knew that it would be fixed and remedied some time later; it was of no concern during the instinctive movements they shared. Carpet real-estate was eventually hard to see as the hurricane had swept pages upon pages to the ground. Fiona followed suit by being lain down amidst the discarded clothing and papers that lined the floor. Jon's jacket enveloped her outline as she lay beneath him. Lowering his head to kiss her and stretching his arms ahead of him as he stayed on his knees, Fiona exhaled a fluttering breath and wrapped her legs around his waist once more.

- You going to get in trouble for this?

He didn't look at her when he spoke, and uttered words between noiseless kisses that traced the curves of her body.

- Probably not, unless someone finds out.
- Yea we wouldn't want that…that would be awful…completely terrible.

She giggled and ran her fingers through his hair. It was soft and short, kept well in check along with his beard. It was rough when it needed to be.

- I love you darling.

It was a shared sentiment; Jon had merely uttered it aloud.

It was Jon who lay beneath Fiona, her hair shielding the light from above and behind her as she eventually squealed and pressed her hands hard into his chest. What hair grew there was tensed and pulled in the process, drawing the sensation in his body in as many different directions as he could handle being that so many nerve endings were wide awake further south. There were few moments in which he felt younger than his wife; here though, she looked after him. The serenity on her face, despite its flushed look, was contagious and Jon was at peace as she got off of him and curled up beside him on the ground. They lay in a two-person-sized snow-angel of papers and clothing for long enough before the cold began to dominate the beauty of what they had achieved and they started up putting their clothes on. Jon helped his wife with each step; he needed to. It wasn't for her. He needed to feel depended on, and he fell more in love with her for letting him be there. She clasped his hand and kissed him hard before bouncing up and assessing the mess that needed fixing. They would emerge from their hideout one after the other at an inconspicuous rate so as to avoid raising the alarm from students passing by who neither cared nor noticed what they had been unknowing parties to on the other side of the glass wall.

---

31 - Fiona – January 17th 6:11pm

Nothing about her experience was quick or painless. Toby's sweaty corpse weighed her down as his hands cuffed her wrists to the ground. His forehead was rooted to the ground beside her face as she stared blankly upwards. His breath was heavy and deep. Each exhale filled Fiona's headspace with the escaping fumes from the toxic human being who had chosen to spend this day destroying something. Fiona was not sure if she could move when her wrists were released from their stocks for humiliation. Toby managed a weak push up from the ground, cold sweat lining his skin wherever it showed. Still a long way from where she lay, Fiona heard the sound of Toby's zipper and belt as he shoved himself away and hastily sought an escape route from the nightmare he'd caused in which he now resided. Fiona breathed as best she could; a chalk outline could have traced the stillness of her body as she lay between the shelves. She uttered what noises she could muster as Toby struggled to his knees with the help of the lower shelves holding various theology and morality periodicals and journal articles from years gone by.

- Toby…

Again he did not hear her. *Perhaps he's as far away as I am. It looks like it was hell for him, too.* She tried again, this time looking up at his face from her resting place through the scattered strands of hair.

- Just go...

Toby left hastily. The sound of his windbreaker shuffling mingled casually with the fluttering of disrupted texts as he swept out of the room. His footsteps were noiseless on the carpet. The glass door latched behind him as he undoubtedly disappeared into the crowd of students who were unaware of the travesty by which they had all walked alongside.

There was immense conflict in Fiona's mind as she lay alone between the shelves. Jonathan, although helping her through her ordeal as it happened, had long since left. *I have to lock the fucking door. I can't be found like this.* She felt rooted to the ground but had no means of mustering the strength to free herself from where she lay. The feeling of her alarm clock having been snoozed repeatedly and her day creeping up on her fast was magnified exponentially as she wrestled in her mind with the urgency of needing to lock the door so she could collect herself in private. She had to mourn the loss of herself undisturbed. *If someone comes in now and I've got my fucking jeans and panties halfway down myself in a crumpled mess on the floor, there is going to be more explaining and procedure than I could possibly handle or deal with or even bear.* Fiona passed a hand over the side of her hair and gradually returned to herself. With a cold efficiency she reached down to her legs and stretched her now deformed and soon to be burned clothing up her thighs and covered herself. Had she been fully aware, the cold sting of what Toby had left behind as the cotton made contact with her would have made her physically sick. After she had zipped her own jeans and wrestled with the button which had been torn and misshapen in the act, the only evidence of it all was concealed in the space between her thighs and between her ears. It was something she would not soon forget.

After grappling to her feet, unassisted by shelves of texts in which she held no faith, Fiona calmly traced her way out of her prison and into the light of her department. It was clinical and cold beneath the buzzing of the bulbs; they seemed louder than they had ever been. She realized quickly she was returning to her senses more and more as she required the use of her body to function. After making sure the door was locked, making eye contact with several oblivious students leaving lectures or making plans for their evenings, she sat at her desk and stared with an unblinking gaze at nothing in particular as her mind rebooted slowly. After not too long, she found herself humming quietly and embracing the reality of the situation. She got out her phone to text Alex, worried about what could have been happening for her earlier in the day. Despite all that had happened to her, she was concerned about what Alex was going through. Alex had promised to call when she could, and no such call had happened. "Thinking about you darling. Hope everything is alright. Glass of wine soon x." The nonchalance of her message was flawless. No rewrite was needed. Any lack of emotion for which she had previously hated text messaging for, was in this case a blessing. Fi sent the message, locked her phone, and gathered her things. The few texts laying out would stay as they were until she returned the following day to do her job.

Fiona made no turn of the head in either avoidance or acknowledgement as she passed the space between the shelves when finally walking out for the night. As soon as the lights clicked off and the door latched behind her she scanned, as always, the window at the end of the hall to judge the weather in preparation for her walk home. *I have to pick up a few bits and pieces on the way. I'm so nearly out of coffee. That would be just a terrible start to the day tomorrow...* She strode from the library, aware of the new aches and pains she felt from her experience, but unhindered by their presence. There were things that needed to be done, and bad things — even the worst of all things — didn't stop the world from turning.

---

32 - Jonathan — January 8th

Unable to stop it from fading, Jon's mind dragged him kicking and screaming away from the library and back to reality. Fiona's skin no longer rested against his, the smell of her hair mingling with the heat created in the air around them dissipated fast as Jon came crashing back to his walk across the campus in the cold. Each frame of what had withdrawn him from his bleak reality ticked further towards one of the blank and empty spots in his mind before disappearing into a black and cloudless void. Tess had vanished into the library long ago. His steps had become laboured as he had absented himself for a brief spell. He picked up his gait and continued his walk around the campus, hearing in the back of his mind his name being called.

- Jon! Jonathan!

Jon turned to see Alex, with her collection of bags, books, and jackets, trotting after him. He waited for her to catch up and she hugged him tightly. She looked as tired as he did and he tried to remember the last time he had seen her but the information had left him.

- How are you doing? How's PhD work? How's Tom?

Jon cared about the answers to the questions and listened to Alex explain herself as she caught her breath from her mini-pursuit. Alex shared something of the loss that Jon felt, but she seemed different, as though rounding the corner of depression had come faster for her with the help of something external or unrelated.

- I'm good yea. PhD is…whatever; but it's getting there. I'll publish one of these days. Tom's fine. He wants to get you out for a beer one of these days.

- Good, good, and yea that would be nice.

There was a modicum of motivation and pep in Jon's voice that had been long since absent after hearing such invitations. Perhaps his most recent spat of daydreaming had lulled his mind into a false sense of security or happiness. Either way, he looked forward to the potential of an evening out with friends for once.

- Is Tom still properly into his beers at the moment? Home brewing and all that?

Alex laughed and tipped her head back, rearranging her hair as she came back down to earth to answer the question.

- Well I put a stop to the idea of home-brewing, but he still takes a good interest in it, yea.
- Well that sounds good, he will have to show me what's good and what's not next time we're out. Could go to that new brew-pub we went to last time.

She looked puzzled for a moment. *Yea she wasn't there that time; that was pretty soon after Fi had left.*

- I think I know the one you're talking about, but it's not exactly new. You've been hiding away for so long Jonathan.

Hearing her call him Jonathan grounded him slightly. It was a moment of confusion in his mind followed by the pangs of pain fluttering through his chest and down his spine as the inflection of her voice had so very much reminded him of Fiona. During the time Fiona had lived in Scotland she had picked up various inflections and tones of the local accent; his name was one that sounded remarkably British for an American girl.

The two talked a little more in the open space of the university quad. It was a flashback for both of them to a time when they had been students. *She's still a student I guess.*

- Well give me a shout and I'll come out to see you guys.

She hugged him tightly and walked away with all of her belongings dangling from her like a Sherpa on an expedition. Jon stood still for a while and turned around to head back to his apartment – his walk had proved to be more fruitful than he'd initially thought it could.

    .. Just a few evenings later, Jon found himself waiting at a round barrel-table at the usual bar. It would be calm. He would drink a few drinks, and walk home unassisted. *None of that nonsense from last time or dad will just about lose the will to live.* Tom walked in and scanned the room, quickly noticing Jon standing by the glass-topped barrel adjacent to the bar. It was crowded considering the early hour. Jon had bought a half-pint of something basic, hoping for insights from his friend – Fiona's friend's husband – about a more appropriate drink with which to continue his evening. Tom signalled that he would head to the bar first as it was busy, and soon returned with two pints of something dark and ominously creamy.

- Cheers mate.
- Cheers.
- Alex joining us later?
- Yea she won't be long. Still at the library believe it or not. I think she works harder than any of us at the moment with the amount of hours she's putting in.
- Well she definitely works harder than I do at the moment.

Jon laughed and took a long drag from his pint as Tom quickly clocked what he meant.

- Yea we were sorry to hear about your job mate.

It was clear that Tom didn't know the whole situation, and Jon was in no mood to retrace the steps he'd taken after having been sacked. He nodded and shrugged off the situation and the two drank slowly for a while before Alex joined them. Tom had asked about Roob; Jon had shrugged it off as well. There was very little to say that would have been acceptable conversation at the time. *Sometimes a shrug is just much fucking easier.* Had Fiona been around, the connection Jon had with Alex and Tom would have been much more tangible and solidified. It would be unlikely that a scenario could exist where Jon could have behaved the way he had and it not got back to Alex and Tom through Fiona. *Women do tend to tell each other everything; especially the wonderfully awful or inconvenient stuff.* He whispered an almost silent cheers to his wife and continued to drink as Tom spiralled on the spot and saw Alex heading in to join them.

Unloading her various books and bags and taking off her winter coat, Alex seemed to shrink to half her original size. She was immediately flushed from the warmth the bar offered and kissed Tom hard before pulling up a stool around the barrel.

- You better not have told him yet.
- I haven't don't worry.

The two smiled. It was obviously good news.

- What's going on guys?

Thankfully not in unison so as to avoid any TV-trope or clichéd vibe, Tom and Alex explained that they were expecting a baby. Jon offered the obligatory congratulations and hugged his friends hard. He slapped Tom on the back and smiled at him. There was a genuine warmth emanating from his face towards his friends at the news that they were creating something together. It was a warmth that had been gone for longer than he had realized. Both Alex and Tom seemed relieved at the response Jonathan gave them. They breathed out hard and relaxed into the various baby-discussions they would be having for the foreseeable future as Tom dutifully fetched Alex another glass of ice-water.

Alex and Tom would undoubtedly leave the evening after having hugged Jon goodbye with happy heads and hearts as their news had been shared to willing ears. They had passed the time comfortably while Tom and Jon sipped beers – all selected by Tom – and talked about Fiona, talked about work, and talked about life. As they left, Jon remained at the barrel a short while to finish his remaining few sips and allow the evening to seep into the spaces in his brain. Everything that he had known to be constant was gone. Fiona's padded steps lining the halls of his apartment, mingling with the sounds of her voice were vanishing into the depths of his memories and would soon reach the edge of a black space into which they would fall. At that point, even *he* would not be able to reach them. He didn't want to think of her as something from the past. She was his present. Only hours earlier, Tom and Alex had seemed the same as they had been during the time when Fiona was just out working still, or unable to join them because she was under the weather. The night had passed with the lolling ease and clockwork of an evening that had happened many times before. *A child, though?*

Had he wanted a child with Fiona? If it had been with anyone it would have been her, but had he wanted a child at all? They were young. They had probably had the discussion at some point during their years together. He couldn't remember clearly what the outcome had been. *It doesn't fucking matter now anyway, does it?* Alex and Tom would disappear into actual adulthood and parenthood. *Fiona would have been by that kid's side perpetually.* Jon paid his tab and left confusedly from the little bar. Despite the beers he'd consumed over the course of the evening, he was as sober as he had been when he had first walked in there. Jon's mind fixed on the translucent and vacant gaze that was so frequently affixed to Fiona's face during his time with her. She looked so peaceful. He wondered if, in moments of serenity or peace or confusion, his own face could mimic such an expression. It did so as he walked home from the bar. His dress-shoes squeaked against his thin socks and rubbed uncomfortably at the skin beneath them. They sent an echoing tap across the cobbled stones of his route home every time his foot fell. *They're having a baby...* Unable to pinpoint in his mind how the news had made him feel, he continued by trying to push the thought as far from himself as he could and instead grapple with the ever-widening spaces that were left by such repression of so many other thoughts that plagued him. His fingers grew cold as he neared his house and he passed his hand over his beard as he walked up the driveway past the *replacement* car that waited so patiently for its next use.

His calmness surprised him as he took off his dark blue trench coat, carefully unlaced his black dress-shoes, and rolled up his sleeves. He stood quietly in the dark of his kitchen and stared through apparently lidless eyes into the expanse that the darkness at the end of the hall offered. Listening carefully, he could not hear Fiona's voice. Assured by the whispering of the wind amongst the leaves outside the kitchen window that it was just quieter than he could perceive, he calmly listened further. A break in the wind allowed the leaves to settle and the kitchen to fall into complete silence. As if heightening his sense of hearing by eliminating his sense of sight, Jon closed his eyes as he stood still and listened. There was nothing to hear. No sound penetrated the thick silence that spread itself across the apartment from one corner or crevasse to the next. *She's gone.*

---

33 - Fiona – January 18th

Fiona had experienced no nightmares upon crawling into bed on the night that she had been used. She had arrived home, still aching and creaking from the torsion and tension of her inside and her outside, with relative ease having collected the things she knew she needed on her way. She would tell someone, eventually. *I'll tell Alex, but it won't change anything.* She had stood in her shower stall with her stretched and bruised clothing still on in her little apartment as the water turned hot down her back, matting her hair to her forehead and allowing it to cling in streams down her neck. Removing each item was a slow and arduous process when wet. Her boots shed the most dirt across the floor of the shower and squeaked under the pressure of her fingers as she wrenched them from her feet. The water was burning hot and perfect. She shoved the boots to the edge of the shower stall and began carefully removing her sweater. It clung to her like a disease fighting for its life until its final fibres severed their contact with her skin and it fell with a heavy splat onto the few millimeters of water lining the floor. Undoing her jeans was as complex as it had ever been thanks to the twisted metal of the zipper. Like the contorted metal framework of a car – their car – that had been forced through an unspeakable ordeal, so too had the mechanism that had so briefly held back Toby's searching fingers. After popping the button and wriggling free, the now darkened blue denim slipped down her thighs and bunched around her ankles in a heavy mess with her underwear in tow.

The hot water served to cleanse and burn away, if only for the night, the experiences of the afternoon and evening. It had the desired effect and Fiona stood with arms pressed against the tiled surface of the shower walls as the water performed its duties admirably. What tears she was sure she must have shed, found their way out without parade or applause as they immediately found themselves caught up amongst the current and torrent of water. It was just the next time she cried without knowing or feeling it; there would surely be times to follow. *I have to tidy up the mess tomorrow at work, I haven't left it like that for a long time. Not since Jonathan and I had our own little escapade.* Small streams of blood emerged in the water beneath her feet. As always the water embellished everything. Fiona carefully examined herself as she washed, each small fleck or cut warranted only a second or two of an extra look. She was fine, really. After finally stepping away from the hot stream of the shower, the cool air seemed to sear and cauterize any final blemishes on her skin before she wrapped herself in a towel and headed for bed. Her clothes lay sopping and darkened in the bottom of the shower overnight. What sleep she enjoyed had been dreamless; her eyes had closed immediately and when they opened after what seemed like seconds, the morning waited aggressively to greet her.

"Hey darling, you coming by work today? Want to make sure everything's alright! x." Fiona's concern for her friend's wellbeing served to distract her from what was going on in her own life. She looked forward to seeing Alex and helping her work through whatever was going on. *I don't even know that there is actually something wrong; it's all been in text. She might be fine or it could just be nothing.* Alex replied during Fiona's morning coffee. It was as any other morning would have been in a Scottish January for Fiona: a little cold and hopelessly supported by a caffeine crutch. It was a short reply "Yea I'll see you in a bit babe!" Fi paced about the house in her morning routine, her coffee mug surgically attached to her hand as though an IV would have been easier by far. She smiled at the pictures of Jonathan lining her walls and looking at her from behind the apps on the screen of her phone, and stayed only partially aware of the new aches and pains she had acquired from yesterday's forced workout.

-   Well… fuck…

Her day would start with the cleaning she had neglected on the previous evening. *I have to make sure this is all gone before Alex shows up… What if Toby comes back, too?* It was something that had not yet crossed her mind. She had imagined he would simply disappear after what he had done, but also realized that she was by no means in the business of knowing what was going through the poor young man's head. *He won't come back.*

Alex tapped hard on the glass and Fi shuffled over to her with an armful of papers and unlatched the door to let her in. It was still about ten minutes before the department opened, but this was normal for Alex. What was peculiar was her lack of books and bags and endless jackets or scarves. She slipped in through the glass door, sat at the long table, kicked her boots off and rested her feet on the wooden surface in front of her.

-   Just own the place, do you?
-   Yea, you know how it is.

The two laughed, but Fiona wanted to know what was going on, first from the night before and now with her lack of work or bags. *Can she tell something happened to me?* Fi quickly squashed the thought as Alex's message had come before Toby.

-   Where's all your stuff? You look like Toby right now.
-   Who is Toby?
-   Never mind. Doesn't look like you're going to be doing any work, though, today darling?

Any remnants of the commotion of the previous evening had been filed away amongst texts and journals that would swallow it into sheltered or hidden ignominy; something that could, as any other piece of work on the shelves, be withdrawn at a later date for further examination. Fi waited patiently for Alex's response as she was texting or emailing.

-   Nope. No work today babe.

She stared with a smug smile at Fiona across the room, as if waiting for the elephant to reveal itself of its own accord.

-   Aren't you going to ask me, then?
-   What?
-   Don't be a bitch!   Yesterday you seemed dead concerned about what was going on.

They laughed and Fiona caved.

-   Okay yea. I was worried about you, sue me. I thought you and Tom had had a ruck or something, but then I realized that was like the least likely thing in the world. *But...* Reuben is also in a committed relationship, so stranger things have happened recently.
-   That's true.
-   So yea, what's up?

Alex was evidently enjoying herself. Fi let her sit in it for a while before screwing up a piece of paper into a ball and throwing it in her general direction.

-   Was that meant to get me?
-   Yea, but you know I can't throw. What's going on?
-   I'm pregnant babe.

Fiona sat back and actually felt the tears welling up in her eyes. They were for the right reasons, perhaps that was why she actually felt them.

After having spent the day not focusing on work or on repeatedly stepping over the invisible chalk outline of her frame between the shelves as the hours passed and she placed different volumes where they belonged, Fi escaped the department and spent the evening alone at the new-ish brew pub not far from the university. Drinking alone was rare for her. *I should be happy for them. I miss him so much. I don't even know if*

that was what I wanted for us, or what he wanted for us. Still, it doesn't ✓
seem fair. Was it fair that he died and I didn't? Would it have been easier
if we had both gone or something like that? She quickly shifted herself
out of the dangerous area of her mind into which her train of
thought did its best to drag her. Tom and Alex's news was
positive. Fair had nothing to do with it; life wasn't fair, but it
was always interesting. Her drink – just one – went down
slowly and eased her nerves as she began to feel anxious. She
felt stressed for Alex and Tom and what they would face.
They were so well equipped to deal with what they faced, but
it was still terrifying. *Should I be feeling more about Toby? I wonder*
where he is. . .

"Looking forward to catching up properly on the
weekend babe." Alex's text brought her back to the bar and
washed the newly forming glaze from her eyes. Her beer was
almost gone and she would head home when it was. *Would*
Toby have done what he had done if Jonathan was still here? Quickly
realizing that her mind was returning to dangerous places, she
finished the remainder of her drink and watched as the beer
suds slipped down the sides of the empty glass as she put on
her coat and scarf. She was happy for Alex and Tom. She
thought slowly, as if in fragments, about how she could tell
Alex about what had happened given the circumstances. It had
happened *one day earlier* but the world already seemed to have
changed beyond recognition since then. It was Jonathan,
amongst everything, who kept her in place and stopped her
from falling out of touch with everything she couldn't control
in her own mind.

Sleeping alone was, for reasons she couldn't entirely
understand, more difficult that night. *Toby maybe?* She pulled
the covers of her bed high around her head and bunched them
tightly around her face, leaving a gap only wide enough to see
and breathe through as she tried to fall asleep. Unlike her

previous night in a dreamless yet comatose state, Fiona tossed and turned while half awake, rendering and squashing various images in her head that led her down the path towards sleep before raising her heart rate and eventually dragging her back to wakefulness. The duvet-fortress was abandoned quickly for every possible position in her bed that could be comfortable, but there was no way she could lie that would adequately replicate the feeling of Jon's chest for her to rest her head on while he pretended to sleep. She knew that it was not comfortable for him to sleep with her head where she always kept it, but he'd never mentioned it. Eventually the demi-nightmare images that laid themselves across her eyes became consistent enough to draw her into a fitful sleep. It was one she would have to get used to and overcome without the comforts to which she had become so accustomed.

---

34 - Jonathan – February 2nd

The cold of the concrete against the side of his face was oddly refreshing. As it was the last thing he would feel, it seemed good. It touched the entire left side of his face, leaving bobbled imprints across his skin and shielding the view from his left eye out of which he instead saw only blackness. The field of view from his right eye was obscured and left him to imagine what he actually beheld. *It's definitely the sky. Scotland knows how to do the sky.* The grey colour the sky offered above where he lay was by no means the best that Scotland could do. It mirrored the grey of his irises. Although his hands lay upturned against the cool ground, the sensation had left them; they were no longer his to control. All such control had been relinquished after he had stepped from the top of the building.

Lying quietly before any passers-by had noticed his predicament, he felt no pain. He did not yet feel the release he'd hoped for that would surely reach him in death. But what was perhaps worse, was that he no longer heard Fiona singing. The quiet he had felt in his apartment had become endless, the vacancy she had expressed in her distinct gaze over the years had now encapsulated the last notes she would utter into his ears. Her voice was neither distant nor quiet, he simply felt its absence. The scars on his back which had plagued him for the months that followed the accident that withdrew him from his life no longer curled or itched against the fabric of his shirt. All feeling was, by this point, merely imagined between his ears. He would shortly die; this was just fine. As he drifted off, the grey of the sky turned to white. The synapses in his brain fired erratically for the last time, producing the final thought that he did not experience the flashing of his life before his eyes as was to have been expected based on what little knowledge he had of suicide.

Jonathan had walked to the roof of the university library building on his last afternoon. It was not busy below as he looked over the edge to see where he would meet the ground. He was irritable and tired. His beard was short but unkempt with no definite beginning or ending to it's span. His hair, where it still grew properly, was as wayward as Roob's had been even without the assistance of the wind. *I wonder if the wind will change how I fall.* His thoughts were absent and indirect. The myriad of things that should have been racing through his mind were elsewhere. The pain in his back from his not-so-new scar was dull but present. It hadn't impeded his walk to the roof of the building and for this he was quietly grateful. He wore comfortable clothes and shoes and felt their fabric flap gently against him in the breeze. It had not crossed his mind that the clothes he wore would be the last in which he would be seen alive. Choosing an outfit in which to die was an odd concept. Choosing the day he would die had not really been a choice. It had just been the *right* day to bring it all to a close. His journey to the university had included a stop for coffee at a small café he had frequented over the previous few years. It was ordinary. He had chatted in passing with the barista who had prepared his drink. His face maintained the angst and turmoil that had caused him to be where he stood atop the building. He had expected a serenity to have washed over him at some point during the morning or the afternoon, as would on the face of a serial killer who calculates his moves and then executes them perfectly. Jon's demeanour was in keeping with how it had been in the year that had led to his footsteps on the roof, no such serenity arose.

He knew he would do it. There was no question that he would make the step out towards nothing. *It'll be like assuming another step exists at the top of the staircase in the dark. No. It'll be like I think I've reached the bottom, only to be surprised by dead air from one more...* Yet, his mind still churned over the trivialities which awaited him back at his desk. The pot that rested next to the kettle was almost empty of teabags. He would need to refill it. The coffee had also been almost empty for too long; prices of both beverages from several different stores in the city sprang into his mind as he unconsciously dealt with the problem. All such thoughts were automatic. He had not left his car unlocked as if he knew he would not be returning to it. The green 3-Series with the grey interior was parked not too far away from the library as he had not wanted to walk far this afternoon. He had paid for the parking in the meter for the rest of the afternoon so as to not receive a ticket. At no point did any thought like *"what would it fucking matter if I had just left the damn car in the middle of the street"* even cross his mind at all. He still parked in the spots in which Fiona knew to look if he was picking her up from work. Someone else had her job just six floors beneath where he stood. Someone else, *Tess I think*, stacked the periodicals and journals in a fashion that would surely have annoyed her beyond belief. Jon was glad she did not have to see that happen.

- This place would fall apart without you darling.
- Don't be silly.
- I'm serious! But you should still quit and go back to school.
- Well then we'd really be skint wouldn't we?
- Of course not, I'd work more or get another job, too. You know that.

It was an awfully long time since he had said anything like that. It had been a long time since he had someone to whom he could say such things. This seemed to be the best he could do under the circumstances; he was sure it was. It had to be, really.

From where he stood on top of the library building he was relatively shielded from view. Very few people knew about the roof access or even had access to it at all. He had ended up there as part of some team-building game years before that had hidden a clue or something there. He had forgotten what the clue was; it didn't matter. Standing on the spot in the wind on the flat roof, Jonathan looked around slowly. He took in his surroundings and breathed calmly under the circumstances, squinting his eyes slightly at the greyness and whiteness that the sky emanated over the day. The library building was high enough for his purposes. Other buildings in the near-distance vaulted several floors above him, but they were not the *right* buildings. It was not clear, just too bright to be pleasant without sunglasses. *What're mum and dad up*

197

to this afternoon, I wonder? I don't really know what they enjoy doing anymore. He thought carefully about his parents and tried to imagine what they would be doing. Geoff would probably be watching TV at home while Clara was on the phone in the kitchen talking to friends and complaining about neighbours or something. His imagination was far from vivid and it irritated him. He wanted to know they were doing something that would make them happy, he just didn't know what that would be. Being unhappy had been of significant detriment to Jon's ability to see others being happy or understand what might make them happy. *That's probably why I'm up here though, right?* It wasn't. He knew what would have made him happy, but Fiona was gone. With her had gone a part of him that he had been unable to make up for.

He had been tired when he'd arrived at Geoff and Clara's house the week before. They had welcomed him in with open arms, and the cut above Geoff's eye had healed over almost entirely, leaving only the tiniest indication on his face that anything had been wrong at all. The surrounding lines of age had creased into a smile upon seeing his son's car come up the driveway. He was uninvited; that was better. Geoff opened the door and stood leaning against the frame as his son walked up the driveway hanging his head.

- Dad, I'm really sorry—
- Don't be a berk, it's alright, come have a drink, eh?

After a pat on the back and a light shove through the door as a dad might give after his son returned hours later than expected from a game of football just down the road, the two men went to the kitchen.

- There'll be none of that nonsense from last time, right?

Clara had a different approach, apparently.

- I know mum. I'm sorry—

She, too, cut Jonathan off before he could get into anything. It was for the best.

- Tea?
- Of course, cheers.

The three stood quietly in the kitchen as the kettle dutifully filled the silence with white noise.

- How's David?
- Oh, he's David. He's onto some new idea or other, but I think he's still doing fine at university for the time being.

If David had been brought up as a conversation filler or subject changer, it had worked. Geoff and Clara talked freely about him. His problems were problems, but they weren't problematic; they just weren't *problems*. David was sensible in that way. Jon was frustrated with himself that he had allowed so much time to pass without contacting his brother, or without knowing what was going on in his life. From what his parents explained, though, he was not the only one with very little knowledge of what or how he was doing. *I'll make sure I give him a ring this week.*

Clara looked hard at her son. She made no effort to hide the concern on her face, however, her years concealed it somewhat and neither Jon nor Geoff commented on her worry. All three were well aware of the situation. It was not clear-cut or easy to deal with by any means, but Jon seemed to be making progress.

- I've missed her every day since she left.

There was no other way that he could express it. He wished he could find the sentence to encapsulate the turmoil and tension that had inhabited his brain since everything had changed. His search for poignancy returned only the simple truth of it all: he missed Fiona, and couldn't find a way to cope. The three talked for hours until they became aware of the darkening sky outside the kitchen window.

- It isn't fair. I know that. You guys know that, too.

His parents mumbled in agreement.

- And yea, I know the whole "life isn't fair" horseshit that people peddle, but it still doesn't change a crap hand.

Jon slowly snuck his arms back into his jacket as it hung on the back of the dining room chair. He shuffled it onto his shoulders and stood up to leave. Part of him knew that his final credits would soon roll, but it did not feel like the last time he would see his parents, so he did not act as though it would be.

- You off then mate?
- Yea. I'm going to try to get a decent night's sleep tonight. I'll ring David this week, too.

This evidently made his parents happy. It was good to know that despite not understanding it, some things he did could still make people smile a little. *To be fair, though, I'm the reason they weren't smiling to begin with, so I guess we'll call it even.*

- It was really nice of you to come over, darling.
- Yea it was good to see you, too, mum.

Jon's parents followed him to the door this time, a markedly different exit from Jonathan's previous one. They hugged and watched him walk down the driveway back to his car, comfortable in the knowledge that he would be ok; that it would all be ok.

Back on the roof Jonathan was deep in thought about very little. The brightness of the sky had left his mind as he meandered towards the edge of the building and placed his hands against the concrete. While not entirely a railing or guard, as the roof was not meant to be frequented by visitors, the edge would require Jon to climb up to it in order to comfortably step from the edge. He waited a while in the comparative safety of the flat roof area. Once he was up there on the edge he would have to step quickly in case people saw him. *Wouldn't want to cause a scene now, would we?* Instead, he stood calmly with his palms flat on the concrete and looked out over the quiet city. The wind worked as a white noise machine for everything on the roof. When he had first opened the service door and stepped out it had been loud but he had soon become acclimatized and enjoyed the relative silence it offered. After several moments more of empty and directionless contemplation, he climbed up onto an indistinct part of the concrete edge. Looking down quickly over the edge of the building he checked to ensure there were no overhanging items he might catch himself on during his descent; no parapets on which he would leave a mess. There were not. It would be just fine. With a more focused approach now, Jonathan scanned the surrounding area to the spot on which he thought he would land. There were very few people around. Classes were in session, but the periodical swell of students occurred near the beginning and ending of each class session. A larger man sat on a bench perhaps 100 yards from the landing site. *Perhaps he will run away when I land — land; did that seem like the right word? Maybe he will be the first one to come over to see what had happened.* All of the other passers-by seemed to be moving away from the landing site or were taking courses that would not cross paths with it. Jon stretched out his left foot, breathed out slowly, and plunged it towards the step that wasn't there—

---

35 - Fiona – February 2nd

Fiona stepped quickly up the path towards Alex and Tom's house. She followed her friend's steps and tried to keep up with the torrent of information pouring from her lips as she strode. *I'm sure Tom is the one who is keeping quietly calm amidst everything.* Fi had run through how she thought the evening might go several times in her head over the previous week. Her quietness in the car on the way was shielded from Alex's awareness by her own abundance of comments, and Fi had politely nodded along with the vacancy in her stare that her friends had come to know as the norm. *I'll tell her everything about Toby. I'll start right from the beginning. She'll overreact — well, she will react how anyone would — and then her and Tom will talk police and all that nonsense. Not going to happen. I need to make sure I bring it up properly so that it doesn't spoil anything, though. They want to talk about the baby. I'll talk about the baby. I'll spend the whole evening talking about the baby, and when things tend towards a slightly more somber or quiet note, ill simply... tell her what happened. I've got to tell someone, right? I guess a lot of people don't. I've just got to not fuck this up. That's what I've got to do...* Despite her best intentions, the evening would only go the way it would go. She would do only what she could.

Tom poured beers in the kitchen, just one for him and one for Fiona, as they walked in.

- Just water for me darling!

He knew. It was just one of the things that Alex was allowed to enjoy about not drinking: she could use it to explain that she was pregnant as often as possible, even to her own husband. True to form, the three talked about babies and pregnancy for longer than anyone should. They were happy. It had evidently not crossed either Alex or Tom's mind to think that Fiona would be anything other than happy about the news or willing to talk about it. In a way, they were right. Inside, though, Fiona was conflicted about how she felt.

There were familiar pangs of jealousy and envy that she wished would just go away. There was relief welling up within her that she didn't have to deal with the kinds of stressors that having a child entailed. Mostly, there was just the same unexplainable sadness that she tried to push downwards and away to file with the books at her work that she would never read, but could do if she ever wanted to.

Alex would have finished her PhD by the time the baby was born. She explained, with a science that was relatively unsolicited, the exact date of conception so far as she knew. They talked about how this baby was *kind of* an accident but also *sort of in the plans*. Fiona was concerned throughout the evening that she was not talking enough; that she didn't show enough overt excitement over their news; that she seemed more afflicted than usual. If she was falling short in any such regard, neither Tom nor Alex picked up on it. *Was that good or bad? I don't want them to just assume I'm sad and pathetic all the time and just have people let it slide as the norm...* Tom got up quickly and excused himself to deal with something or other for work, and Alex cracked open another bottled water.

- So what's new with you, babe? You've been sat listening to us talk about literally *one* thing all bloody evening and most of this week by text. I've been a bit of a shit friend.

Fiona laughed and shrugged off the comment.

- You're not a shit friend in the slightest.

If ever the opportunity to actually talk about her problems were to present itself, this was that time.

- Some stuff I guess.

Alex flashed a half smile, sensing the intrigue of the situation. It quickly faded as she read the lines of Fi's face and saw that whatever *stuff* was going on might not actually be all that great.

- Explain yourself babe.

- It's been a pretty long week. It's been really nice to hear about you guys' news though to take my mind off things and keep me sane. I'm probably looking forward to it as much as you guys are.

It was clear to Alex that Fi was trying to smooth something over. She appreciated the sentiment that Fiona was happy for them about the baby, but was far more concerned about what was going on before. She spoke directly as she questioned her friend.

- What's going on Fi?

She breathed out and put down her tea. Beers had long since been abandoned for the evening and the two women, as if in some sort of show of solidarity, were enjoying non-alcoholic drinks. Bracing herself for the response that would pour from Alex's mouth in what would almost definitely be ninety percent profanity, Fi began to explain herself.

- This week; that day that I thought there was something wrong between you and Tom, right?
- Yea.
- I... was calling you. Because I did my application.
- What.
- Yea. Most of it anyway... I still need your help with the rest.

She had bailed out of explaining herself. She didn't really know why, but it didn't seem to matter in the end. Whatever awkward silence she had expected as Alex would examine her to see if she was telling the truth did not happen. It seemed that she could keep Toby's mistake to herself. Her "news" pacified Alex's curiosity and sparked a conversation that led to probably as many probing questions as the truth would have.

Alex worked her way through the basic questions as she knew the process, and Fiona came up with answers that fit as they went along. She realized, halfway through the conversation, that she was actually planning the PhD program she had wanted to start for years. *Did it take a lie to actually get this started? I have to do it now. I have to at least make the application as I have explained to Alex so that I can make truth out of my lie. So I'm doing this now, I guess.* It must have made her happy without realizing as she soon spread a slight smile across her lips while listening to Alex talk about her options. Toby was far from her mind. Jonathan was smiling at her. He was proud. He had wanted her to do it for so long. *He doesn't have to do two jobs or anything for me to do this. Still can't believe he offered that.*

- Jonathan would have been so proud of you eh, babe?
- I know. He really would.

Wherever Toby was, what he had done to Fiona was quickly disappearing. He had left her mind. She would eventually be able to look back at that day and wonder whether she had been strong. She would be able to look more closely at how she dealt with everything. As she chatted with Alex over a cooling cup of tea, though, she thought only about Jonathan, and about the conversation she would have had with him about the future he wanted for her. *Perhaps it was time to actually get started? I have to now. I want to.* She tucked her legs beneath her on the couch in Alex and Tom's living room and allowed the make-believe situation to become true in her own mind. It would come to life as she followed the instructions she had spilled forth to her friend as though they were already in the past. She was happy; happy with herself. Missing Jonathan was inevitable. *This*, however, would make him happy if he could have ever known.

---

36 - Jonathan – February 2nd – 2:07pm

Falling took a great deal longer than he had expected. The spot on which he would soon be resting and feeling the ground beneath him for the last time seemed further away than it was. *Maybe something happens to our brains' concept of time during a situation of impending doom.* He by no means approached the speed of light, but the space-time of his journey from the roof to the ground was also by no means conventional. The space before him seemed to retract and expand and shift and tilt in ways he had not seen before. He turned over a little in the air as his right shin and foot had clipped the edge of the building as he had left it. He was falling to the ground, however quickly or slowly, in an open belly-flop like a child at the pool who had bailed out of a front flip attempt and must brace for the red stomach that would soon follow the mistake. His arms trailed somewhat behind the weight of his body

Fully formed and well articulated thoughts about Fiona came and went during the journey. Such thoughts would have taken hours of musing under normal circumstances. Instead of a life flashing before his eyes that had already happened, he imagined a different one. *Was it a future? Was it just something that had existed elsewhere or never existed due to circumstances of any given event?* His mind grappled with the countless images that flowed through its field of conception as they slowed or sped up uncontrollably. Some thoughts were formulated with the brain power of a man in his sleep capable of dreaming days or weeks of activity in just a few seconds or minutes of real-time. Others were a flash; a flash of Fiona's face, older than he had ever seen it, partially covered by her hair in a style he did not recognize. The corners of her smile and the shape and colour of her eyes were the same. It was unmistakeably her. He knew his wife better than he knew himself. *Is this how I'd have seen her in ten years' time?* She was beautiful nonetheless, but was soon replaced by another fleeting image.

Flashes continued to replace one another; Reuben was getting married, or something. He looked smart; only slightly older. He was not from Jonathan's past as far as he could remember. Reuben smiled a half-formed smile; probably the best he could do under whatever circumstances. *Do I know what's happening there?* Reuben quickly disappeared, replaced by images of his parents in their later years, by his brother in his thirties with a small child, by Alex and Tom at their child's graduation from something or other. Everyone's life went on. Tom stood with a stoic expression that Jon did not recognize over an unfamiliar scene. Alex was tired, but evidently content. They looked as they should. Each flashing image was forgotten as quickly – or slowly – as it was conceived and Jon slipped back momentarily into an awareness of his journey to the ground. The spaces in his mind that had for months been black, empty spaces were full of a white noise that burned inside his head. Someone was turning up the volume to its maximum on a TV-channel broadcasting only static. Soon the sound was replaced by the noise of the elements passing him on his way down; the few flashes that still made it to the projectionist in his mind's eye were exclusively Fiona. Unable to properly understand what he was seeing behind his eyes he began to quickly return to the present and to the gravity of the situation. Jon felt the wind against his face as he rushed to the ground now with a more urgent sense, apparently finding some different plane or wavelength in whatever was occurring in his mind on what was probably, at most, just a handful of seconds of descent. *Is this going to hurt? Fuck, probably. Might not, though? Probably be over pretty instantly—* Fiona.

There was some kind of commotion nearby. He could hear it vaguely. It sounded far away at first, but the field of white that had been visible from one eye was being passed over periodically by dark shapes. They passed from left to right and back the other way randomly. One seemed to get larger and smaller, and more distinctly black and dark as it grew. It faded as it shrank and eventually disappeared, replaced once more by the white field that Jonathan was convinced was the colour of the Scottish afternoon sky. The noises, too, were indistinct. They must have been voices, but there were no words he could understand clearly. They seemed to reach his damaged ears from behind a great deal of division or insulation between he and the source. The inflection at the end of each utterance changed its volume and each swelled and then waned to a dull hum before disappearing entirely or being replaced by the start of another. *It's people. There must be people around me.* The thoughts reached his mind in similar fashion to the shapes and sounds that surrounded him. They were dull and ill-formed. Last. Final. They didn't stutter or reach clarity like a loading picture or poor connection. They instead seemed crude and rough edged. Soft in the impact they would have on his brain, they used the fewest possible firing synapses that remained, until the last thoughts meant nothing at all. The shapes disappeared; the white disappeared. The sounds ceased. Everything was gone.

Various shrieks and outbursts of shocked profanity were the first sounds to reach Jon's body that would just bounce off of him. A gentleman who had been eating his lunch on a bench minutes earlier was now stooped over the body and was doing his best to remember what he could about first aid or how to check someone's pulse. In the excitement of the situation it seemed apt to keep hidden that his knowledge in such a field was exclusively limited to what he had seen on television or learned a long time earlier in a P.E class in high school.

- He's got no pulse.
- No. That's really fast. You must be doing it wrong.

Another bystander moved the bigger man out of the way and tried his hand at finding any signs of life from Jonathan.

- Is anyone calling a fucking ambulance, too?

As if in sync, the group of observers fumbled for their phones until someone announced that an ambulance was on its way.

- Yea. He's got no pulse.
- Told you.

The second man scowled hard at the first. No argument arose, though. It was clearly neither the time nor the place. Several people from the background of the small crowd that had formed within minutes had started to walk away from the scene and continue with their lives. Jonathan's final adventure would be, to them, nothing more than an unpleasant story they would tell at pubs and gatherings for years to come, commenting on how sad it was that someone could think that suicide was the only option. They would remark on his decision like they knew him. They would prescribe a backstory and history for the young man who took his life. They would judge his decision and explain the many alternatives he had, explaining their charming tales of many other people they knew who were in a low place or suffered depression but had been a success story and walked out of the other side of their problems. They would *know* him in their stories. Several days later on the news, when Jon's name would be released, they would have the final piece of the story that they would perfect throughout years of telling and re-telling down the road.

After several minutes of the group declaring that Jonathan must be dead, they stood in silence and tried to ensure that no more crowd gathered around his body.

- How long does it take for an ambulance to get here, then? Or the police… or something.

The man's voice was genuinely inquisitive. The group shared the same feelings of anxiety and confusion mixed with concern and fear. It was a strange limbo in which they found themselves. What was the protocol for sticking around in such situations? What normally happened between the time the body hit the ground and the time the ambulance showed up? On TV it was an instantaneous occurrence; one promptly followed the other and then the body was whisked away as the music was queued and ominous tones encapsulated the scene. Several members of the small crowd turned their heads and followed with their eyes the route that several of the abandoners had taken. They had made the right choice in leaving. There was a sense of social responsibility and selfish intrigue that mingled in the minds of each observer as they stood on the concrete square by Jonathan's twisted body. His legs were splayed oddly behind him, both shoes remained tied firmly to his feet, but the directions his feet pointed made the onlookers ill at ease. His clothes were relatively intact considering his journey. They resembled the dishevelment of the clothes of a man who had taken the redeye to his destination. Despite their damage and wear, they concealed the battery his body had experienced on its last journey. This was for the better of the onlookers regardless of their intrigue.

- Does he have a phone on him? Or like, a wallet or something?

People turned to face the speaker in the crowd with a confused look. He quickly understood the frightening ambiguity of his statement and clarified.

- No. Not to nick or anything. Like, to see who he is. Or like, we could call someone.

Several people murmured in agreement.

- Yea but maybe we shouldn't touch or disturb him or anything. I don't know how this shit works.

In the distance, the sound of sirens was beginning to become clear over the wind and city noise.

- Yea. Don't touch him. The cops or paramedics will do it. Nobody really has to stick around, too. As long as there's a few people who saw the whole thing.
- Did you?
- Yea I was just over there having lunch when he fell.
- Fell?
- I don't know, jumped. Stepped? It doesn't fucking matter to us, does it?

Police cars pulled up and took over quickly, taking over for the man whose lunch had been interrupted and ensuring that people stayed back an appropriate distance. The ambulance was fast in tow and Jon's body was quickly shielded from view. The crowd quickly dissipated and left just the larger man talking with the police officers and paramedics. He gave his statement and left his information.

- There was no way he fell by accident. I don't even know what he would have been doing up there. As far as I know, you can't even open the library windows anyway; so, he *must* have been on the roof.

Geoff and Clara's phone rang first. Clara shrieked and slipped to the ground, squeezing the plastic phone until her knuckles whitened. Geoff stumbled where he stood, as though something vital inside him that had once been helping him to stand had been whisked away without warning. He stabilized himself against the kitchen counter and coughed loudly.

Grasping the phone from his wife's hand, he dealt with the police officer on the other end of the line.

- We have tried to contact a Mrs. Fiona Platt as Mr. Eliot had been in most frequent contact with her but as of yet we have been unable to do so.
- Yes…um...well—
- Is there any way you could contact her sir? Sir?

Unable to comprehend what was happening, Geoff meandered through the impossible phone conversation as the woman on the other end of the line did her best to explain the situation and at least cauterize Geoff's wounds a little. He was slowly able to explain that Fiona would not be available for them to contact, but that he and his wife would go wherever they needed to go to see their son. It was far away from him; the entire conversation. Everything became hazy and unfinished in his mind as he did his best to hold things together with the success of trying to cup water in one's hands. Something left him as he hung up the phone and let it slide from his hand and clatter across the kitchen counter. It was the second time in as many months that Jonathan had sent him to the ground.

---

37 - Fiona – March 17th

It was done. She had managed to finish it off so quickly. Whatever had been holding her back for years had released its grip and she had finished her application to the program. *Could be the start of something really good... Or it could fall pretty flat if I get flatly rejected.* She knew she wouldn't find out for a long time if she was successful, but it gave her cause and reason to get up every day aside from the daily routine that simply served to remind her of Jonathan's absence. In some ways, she felt as though she was embarking on the journey *for* him. It wasn't the case, of course. It was for her, but it felt like the right thing to do in his eyes, too. Her whole field of vision and perspective had added a slight sense of grayscale over the previously sepia-toned or washed-out view that she had donned since he'd died. It was his eyes. *It must have been his view.*

- How are you doing this morning darling?

Geoff's voice was quiet and calm as he drove. They had been in and out of the car all morning. He'd apparently been around and not too busy so he had offered to help her get her application together, print things off, and submit it all to the office in person at the university. It had actually been a great help as it was raining hard. Geoff's wipers did their best to keep up with the torrential downpour, but it was best to just keep their meandering pace as they had ticked off the various things that needed to be done. Fiona had exhaled deeply after handing over the dossier of information to the admissions office in person. It was, quite literally, out of her hands at this point.

- I'm really good actually. I'm excited for lots of reasons. Haven't felt like that for a while.
- What do you mean?
- Well. Since Jonathan died, it's been so hard to look forward any further than just making it to work or getting groceries for home. Now Alex is pregnant, Roob is being an adult, and I've got my application to think about. Things are kind of keeping on and I get to be a part of it. I want to be a part of it I guess.

She had become much more candid when speaking about Jonathan. Geoff murmured in agreement. He seemed to have been doing okay, but had slowed down since February and couldn't really pinpoint why. Something had changed.

213

Perhaps it had been long enough since Jonathan had died that things were starting to feel even minutely normal. This was terrifying. Fiona thought about when relationships in the past had ended for her and the scariest or most daunting moments came six months or a year afterwards when the realization that life kept going started to sink in. A life shouldn't keep going after certain things, but it always did when it was unwelcome. Such weirdly positive thoughts only arose because things were going okay though, right?

Through her new grayscale-bluetone view, she looked hard at Geoffrey Eliot's face while he drove. He smiled awkwardly when he noticed and she laughed at him and looked away.

- I'm going to go to see Jonathan this week again. It's been a while since I've been up there and I want to make sure everything is still ok there.

Geoff turned to look at her.

- I thought you didn't like it there?
- I don't.

Fiona was honest, but it wasn't because she didn't miss him. It was precisely the opposite.

- It's always been a bit surreal for me up there. Or a bit real... I guess I don't really know how it makes me feel, but it's not what I like.
- Okay.
- Yea. But this time I have things that I want to tell him... Or just say out loud. And I think it would be the right way to do it.

Her father in law nodded in approval. He was about to offer a lift but realized quickly in his head that she wouldn't accept it. Going to see Jonathan in such a way was clearly something she wanted to do by herself. Even if he waited in the car park it wouldn't be the same for her.

They neared Fi's house after their morning of errands. She was excited about the future. It was eerie to feel like that and she felt guilty for looking forward to something so impacting when Jonathan couldn't be a part of it. She was looking forward to seeing him and telling him properly; as properly as she could, given the circumstances. Looking through the grayscale, she understood that if he could know, he probably already did.

-   Have you told your mother yet about this application and things?

Geoff's tone conveyed that he really didn't quite understand how exciting or serious this was for Fi. She understood.

-   Clara? I sent her a text today. I'll definitely be over to see you guys at your house soon, too. And my mom, yea I'll give her a ring tonight for sure. It'll be morning for her by then so I wont be interrupting her.

Geoff smiled and tried to conceal it a little under the lines of his face. It had been much easier to do over the past five years or so as his age had deepened the blanket under which he could hide how he really felt. Everything simply came across as a practiced stoicism if he wanted it to. He was happy that Fiona had considered Clara to be "mum" even if it had just been for his benefit. Fiona missed the smile and looked ahead; past the pulsing wipers to the washed out view of her building.

Fiona gathered her things from the car and said thanks and bye to Geoff. They both understood how lucky they'd become to have each other through Jonathan. Fiona had never needed looking after, but having Jonathan and Geoff to do it anyway gave her a sense of purpose that she understood only as she got older. Some people needed people to need them. Helping on a sort of anti-altruistic plane. Jon had it, and he'd definitely inherited it from Geoff. She loved them both. She also knew that however somber or serious the morning had

215

been with her grieving father-in-law, it would all be countered by a peculiar afternoon with Reuben and Karen. *They're still going, surprisingly.* She quickly felt bad for adding the "surprisingly" even in her mind. Reuben was doing well. There seemed to be less of a need to see him the way she had seen him before Jonathan had died. *Maybe that's how Jon knew him? Or maybe he saw something different in him.* He seemed so different, in the space of just a few months, to the man who had awkwardly stooped over Jonathan's comatose body in the hospital the week after the accident. It would be good to see them. The walk from the car to the front door of her building was short but windy, sweeping morsels of the ground towards her eyes and drawing water from them in an all too familiar way. Her phone vibrated with another text update from Alex. Her business-style of texting and emailing had seamlessly transitioned into the same rate and frequency of updates, only now they were exclusively baby or pregnancy oriented.

A few days after her big application day and after Alex had explained how proud she was a few hundred times between baby comments, Fiona walked quietly up the white crushed-stone path of the cemetery. It was warm for March; her long skirt blew around her legs as she walked and several bold stones made their way between her toes or between the leather of her sandals and her feet. She hadn't brought flowers with her. *I'm not sure he would have liked it if I had, really.* The cemetery was another strange place for her because she had never been there with Jonathan when he was alive. Riding the bus down a road to the cemetery was something that, it seemed like, all the other passengers were doing alone, too. Unlike the airport, though, she was by far the youngest. Several old men had been sat quietly on the bus in scattered seats. They required no phones or distractions from their task on this occasion; they instead sat quietly and courteously on the bus as the air brakes breathed and sighed on their way up towards the final stop for each of them. *It always seems like a cemetery is on a hill...is there a reason for that? Do people always want to end up on a hill?* She had a strange image in her mind of feeling uncomfortable in her final wooden box on a comically steep and rounded cartoon hill, struggling for air several feet beneath the ground. She slipped from one end of the box to the other as the pitch of the hill was too steep to lie comfortably. The blood would have rushed to her head had she been up the other way; that was fortunate at least. When she finally escaped the box and broke free onto the surface of the cartoon cemetery hill, she stood for a second and faced the top, her head switching directions a hundred and eighty degrees at a time thanks to her eerie, two-dimensional daydream space. Quickly, however, she lost her balance and tumbled down backwards, rolling and bumbling past headstones and flower arrangements as she fell. The image eventually tottered out of her mind as she apparently reached the bottom of the hill and the bus reached the entrance to the cemetery.

The few passengers who remained on the bus as it pulled into the layby were, as Fiona had figured, the older gentlemen in their suits and hats. They were probably less formally dressed than they seemed to Fiona, but it was a pleasant thought to imagine them in such a way. Her fantasy of these *proper* British gentlemen was continued, at least for a short while, as they all allowed her to disembark first. Fiona nodded thankyou to each of them and to the bus-driver as she carefully stepped down. Upon reaching Jonathan's small grave plot several minutes later, she took off her sandals and shook the straggling stones free. Her feet felt as though they'd been wetted by the grass but it was just dry and cold. She laid down her scarf and sat cross-legged in front of Jonathan's plot.

- Hey. I've missed you so much babe.

She carefully rearranged her dress around her bum and around her legs, tucking it in between her thighs so the wind wouldn't take it halfway through her visit and give the rest of the scattered congregation a show. It had been a long time since she had been able to play in such a way with Jonathan; such risky behaviour had always been fun. Looking around, she saw that she was far from anyone else in the cemetery. She would be able to talk freely. As freely as she could, anyway.

- It's been a long few months darling.

The wind picked up as she spoke and it served to quickly let her know that her eyes had begun to water a little. She was informed by the rivers that cooled as they traced their way slowly down her cheeks; still she smiled.

- I've done my application babe. It's all out of my hands now. I'm going to go down to a few days a week if I get accepted. You won't have to take on extra work, though.

She laughed to herself as she gasped for air a little between sobs while she spoke. She didn't know how to feel. The pain in her chest returned and she hurt inside with a feeling of endlessness. There was no way to make it go away. It stretched and pulled inside her as she breathed and did her best to calm herself. She wiped her eyes and continued, Jonathan's gray square-plot of granite staring up at her while she did.

- Yea... It's really been hard without you. Everyone is doing their thing; you know? Alex and Tom are having a *baby!* That really threw me when they told me, but I'm really happy for them.

She told him everything: how Geoff and Clara had been, how Kathy was doing overseas and that she still said she missed him, how David was doing at university, how all their friends were doing. She talked about work and about her PhD proposal. She explained how was nervous, but that it was good.

- Something happened, though. It's the only thing that's happened since I knew you that I was glad you were not here for.

Crying openly in the cemetery was not uncommon. She was sure that hers were not the only tears shed there that day, but was also fairly sure that the reason behind hers was markedly different to many of the others.

- I don't think he meant to darling. He was so scared. I was so scared, though. I saw you that day, too! You were there with me between the shelves. Again!

She laughed as she remembered the adventure she'd had with Jonathan some time earlier.

- I didn't know what to do. I still don't I guess. *But,* you're the only one I've told.

It had clouded over in the time she had talked. More time had passed than she had realized but she kept going despite the cold and the approaching clouds.

- I'm really scared. Things are moving forward and I'm getting swept along with them. I've got to be though. I can't just let things stop. I miss you every day.

The skin beneath her eyes and on her cheeks was reddened by her wiping her tears away. She hoped they would stop soon. She couldn't keep crying like this.

Fiona sat quietly by Jonathan's plot with her hand resting on the gray granite surface as it had done over his hand on the gearstick on the last night she had spoken to him. She gently passed her thumb back and forth over the cold surface until it became warm beneath her skin from the touch. Her knees and ankles grew numb as she sat for so long. The gentlemen who had ridden the bus with her had gone long before and been replaced by a new group without Fiona even noticing; everything just kept going.

- Okay.

She paused and shifted up onto her feet into a squat beside his plot. Her fingers still grazed the granite.

- I've got to go darling. I love you so much.

Her sandals swayed from her hand as she walked next to the path towards the bus stop at the end of the road at the bottom of the hill.

---

38 - Jonathan – February 10th

Pictures of Jonathan and Fiona lined the room as people from both their lives milled around solemnly in groups. Kathy sat quietly alone at her table, watching the procession of people she did not know go by her. It was a position to which she had become accustomed since Fiona's father had been long gone. Geoff and Clara had watched various people filter through the room for some time before signalling to Reuben that it was probably time to start soon. Their faces could not be described; blank at best. Everyone would need to move further into the next room of the crematorium. Nobody understood why or how they were there. The year that had passed had changed everything for the families involved and this was apparently how it ended. Very few words were uttered by Jon's family. Murmurs filled the room and the evidence of the chasm between the two age groups of the guests was clear. It seemed more apparent that this was a funeral for a young person.

Uncharacteristically in any sense of how Jonathan would have known him, Reuben Crowell stood confidently ahead of a room full of people who awaited his words. The usual coughs and buzzes of cell-phones that had been politely turned to silent-mode or vibrate could be heard across the small hall. He'd not brought any papers or cards from which to read, and stood with a sense of comfort in his footing that suggested he needed no such crutch, despite the intended length of what he planned to say. Reuben turned and leant over the closed casket and murmured something quietly before standing several feet away from the podium and placing his hands gently in his pockets before he was ready to speak. It was an odd feeling to be watched by an entire collection of eyes that had been double-glazed with a thin layer of moisture throughout the day and preceding week. They saw him, but perhaps not clearly. Reuben's gaze as he opened his mouth to speak was not fixed anywhere in particular. He was well aware of where most of the people he knew were sitting. His eyes might pass across the corridors of their gazes towards him at some point throughout his eulogy, but he doubted he would take stock or notice of it as they did.

- I heard an expression somewhere once. Probably more than once if I'm honest.

He paused to ensure that he had found the appropriate pitch and volume. He looked about and straightened his stance a little, shifting the weight from one foot to the other just once.

- It's about life and the way we do our best to navigate our way through it. I'll get it wrong if I try to remember it or read it exactly, but the idea of it is sound. I think so anyway. Life is defined not by the things that happen to us, but by how we choose to react or to respond to them. Those things, those choices, are just about everything. The theory that there is somehow an infinite number of parallel universes existing beyond the reaches of current

221

human understanding suggests that there is, in fact, a universe in which every possible outcome from every possible situation is happening, and has always happened. Endless outcomes with endless possibilities, then. I'm aware that this has the tendency to guide people through their lives in a variety of different ways. Some of us may prefer to believe that we exist on the darkest of all possible scenarios, a "murphy's law" universe in which all of the bad things happen to us; in such places people feel slighted or backhanded in some way. There are also those of us who choose to believe that good things happen and that there is some kind of plan.

Reuben quickly glimpsed at the crowd with a more focused eye as he paused again and readied himself to continue. He noticed that, in the process of speaking, his hands had drawn out of his pockets and assisted his words. They were almost holding them up in front of him for the room to see. He hoped they would be clearly understood.

- Most people, or those who have never actually thought about the possibility that anything other than what did happen has happened, tend to rest somewhere in the middle of this spectrum of good and bad. They rest comfortably in blissful ignorance of the unfathomable number of alternate paths their lives could have taken as they bumble through life doing their best to make the *right* decisions. I honestly don't know where I stand on that line.

There were murmurs about the room in quiet and indecipherable tones. Reuben had thought this would likely be the case. *How do you write and speak a eulogy for someone who didn't want to live anymore when his parents, his friends, and his life sit across the room essentially confused? That's just it, though. His life, as he*

222

knew it, isn't here anymore, is it? I think he died when she did. Reuben realized he had paused long enough this time. He stepped onwards.

- What so many people seem to forget when they have this weird discussion, though, is that such an enormous collection and portrait of possibilities is made larger still by the knowledge that human beings can do very little to influence their surroundings. We think we have control, and we do our level best every day to assert that control over whatever we can so that we can feel like we are doing the *right* thing. What sucks, is that we get so fucking scared when something goes wrong, or when we lose the control that we thought we had when we never really did at all. Most people assume their lives are governed and dictated by the decisions they make, when the scary truth is that they have even less control than that. Life is affected every moment of every day whether a decision is made or not. Our surroundings, our place in time, our specific spot in the universe accounts for an infinite number of possibilities every fraction of every second.

He sped up through his words and what had been clear and powerful enunciation now became an even more powerful emotional framework on which each statement rested.

- Jon did what so many of us would have done in his situation. He thought he had control, some grasp, over it all. He did his best in an impossible situation. To say others have done better or would have done better is irrelevant. They wouldn't have or couldn't have. It's not the same. With this collection of endless outcomes and possibilities, comes the knowledge that every situation is different. Some are incredibly similar, but none of us – none of us at all –

can say that they could know how anyone felt in any such situation. We do our best and that's all we can do. Jon always did that. Then, when it was pointed out to him that he didn't... that he couldn't control anything; when we all lost Fiona—

He paused again, inhaled sharply and rested his hands back in his pockets. The room was quiet and unmoving.

-   That changed everything.

THE END

Made in the USA
Charleston, SC
23 May 2016